Andrew Woods

OXFORD GRAMMAR 6

Name: _____

Class: _____

OXFORD
UNIVERSITY PRESS
AUSTRALIA & NEW ZEALAND

CONTENTS

OXFORD UNIVERSITY PRESS

UNIT 1.1 Common nouns

The Claw

1 Deep in the cellar of the old mansion, the Claw stirs.

2 Slowly the five-fingered talon creeps to the cellar door.

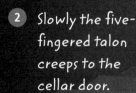

4 Up the stone stairs the terrible creature climbs until ...

3 A key twists in a lock. A handle turns. The door creaks open.

EEEEEEEE

5 ... it reaches the library where, there in an armchair, her back to the door, reading a book and unaware of the approaching danger, sits Arabella Fraser-Smythe-Allan.

7 ... scratches Arabella's terribly itchy back.

6 Silently the fiendish hand moves towards the unsuspecting damsel. Suddenly, with fingers extended, the Claw reaches forwards and ...

OOOH

How's that, Miss?

SCRATCH SCRATCH

Ooooh! Lovely Claw. Just the right spot!

OXFORD UNIVERSITY PRESS

A common noun is a word used to name ordinary things. For example: *table, tree, egg*

1 Write common nouns from 'The Claw' comic strip using these clues.

a   I can be found on a door or a drawer. I am used to open them. _____

b   I am a series of steps. _____

c   I am a possible cause of harm or injury. _____

d   I am a collection of books. _____

e   I am an old-fashioned word for a young woman. _____

f   I am an underground room used to store things. _____

g   I am a huge house. _____

h   I am used to open a lock. _____

i   I am a comfortable chair with arms. _____

There is a noun for every person, creature, place, thing, idea, feeling or quality. Everything that exists can be named using a noun.

Common nouns only begin with capital letters if they are used to begin a sentence.

2 Write a sentence for each of these common nouns.

a   astronauts _____

b   thunder _____

3 Write five common nouns for each group.

a   living creatures _____

b   things that fly _____

CHALLENGE

In your workbook or on a computer, sort the common nouns into the categories shown on the right.

Common nouns			Category	
sadness	saucepan	courage	person	quality
soldier	zoo	thought	creature	idea
shark	teacher	love	place	feeling
curiosity	dragon	anger	thing	
home	flower	jealousy		
octopus	pencil	justice		

Monday blues

Cornflakes were soggy.
Cat licked my egg.
On the school bus
got thumped by Greg.

Sprung again talking
before morning bell —
that Mr Moore can
sure make life hell!

Ticked off for homework —
half out of ten.
Had to miss recess
and do it again.

Strife in mathematics
with Mr Moore.
Sent out to stand in
the corridor.

Looking for battle
came Tracey Frost.
She packs a wallop!
(So guess who lost.)

Biro leaked black ink
on my new jeans.
Soggy fish sandwich
instead of baked beans.

In art and craft room
upset the glue.
Half in my pocket,
the rest in my shoe.

Afternoon playtime,
Shane (my ex-mate)
spread it around that
I fancy Kate.

Practised my footie,
kicked ball quite far.
Guess where it landed?
Mr Moore's car.

Kept in for giggling.
Got home real late.
No wonder bears choose
to hibernate!

by arrangement with
Robin Klein, c/– Curtis Brown
(Aust) Pty Ltd

OXFORD UNIVERSITY PRESS

Common nouns name ordinary things. For example, *bell*, *ball*, *recess*, *battle* and *pocket* are some of the common nouns that have been used in the poem on page 6.

1 Use a noun from the box to describe each group of common nouns.

> food   animals   transport   stationery   clothing   places

a   bears   fish   cat _____

b   jeans   shoe   scarf _____

c   sandwich   baked beans   egg _____

d   car   bus   bike _____

e   corridor   room   playground _____

f   biro   ink   glue _____

Proper nouns are special names of people, places or things.
A proper noun always begins with a capital letter.

2 Write five proper nouns from the poem 'Monday blues' that are the names of people.

_____

_____

> Some nouns can be abstract nouns. They are names for things that you cannot see or touch. For example: **fear, pity, fun, fury, idea, beauty, length, duty, dancing**

3 Find and write these common or proper nouns from the poem.

a   schoolwork done at home _____

b   brand of cereal _____

c   a passageway _____

d   a feline animal _____

e   a teacher at the school _____

f   the writer's ex-friend _____

4 Write proper nouns to match the statements.

a   Usually I am the first day of the school week. _____

b   the capital city of Australia _____

c   the highest mountain in Australia _____

d   the city of the 2024 Olympic Games_____

A collective noun names a group of things or people.
For example: *a **bunch** of grapes, a **pack** of wolves, a **fleet** of ships*

5 Write collective nouns that would be used for these groups.

a   sheep _____

b   bees _____

c   football players _____

d   bananas _____

e   wolves _____

f   cattle _____

CHALLENGE

Here are some unusual *collective nouns*: a **clowder** of cats, a **murder** of crows, a **knot** of toads, a **smack** of jellyfish, a **parliament** of owls, a **business** of ferrets. Imagine that you have been given the job of coming up with collective nouns for the following groups. On a separate piece of paper or on a computer, write or type your suggestions.

a   a ... of clowns

b   a ... of dragons

c   a ... of racing cars

d   a ... of slugs

e   a ... of politicians

f   a ... of mobile phone users

The diary of
Captain Justin Case

We set forth on   (a)   the fifteenth day of   (b)   in the year 1790. Admiral   (c)   , my commanding officer, had requested that I take a crew of five and sail north in search of a suitable place to establish a new settlement. Accompanying me were Lieutenant   (d)   , Sergeant   (e)   and seamen   (f)   ,   (g)   and   (h)   .

Our small boat, named   (i)   , had enough provisions to last five weeks.

We sailed from the safe harbour of   (j)   at 5 a.m. and began our northward journey in fair conditions.

After 20 miles of smooth sailing we passed through the narrow mouth of a reef, about which swam all manner of brightly coloured fish. We have named the passage   (k)   .

We decided to throw out the sea anchor and wait until morning before proceeding. During the night   (l)   caught a live turtle, which he has decided to keep as a pet — he has given the creature the unusual name of   (m)   .

At first light we weighed anchor and sailed towards a small land mass to the east. The island proved to be uninhabited and without fresh water. The island's one dominant feature was a mountain which from some angles resembled a human skull. We have named the island   (n)   and its mountain we decided to call   (o)   .

We sailed directly from the island westward to the mainland where we encountered a wide river mouth, which we sailed into with some nervousness as we could see upon the nearby banks several huge saltwater crocodiles. We felt that an appropriate name for this river would be   (p)   .

After eight miles of river cruising, we decided to make camp for the night. I organised watches in case there were dangerous animals about.   (q)   took the first watch and I took the early morning shift.

A new day and new discoveries.

We trekked inland from our campsite passing through a mosquito-infested swamp ((r)   ), along a dry and rocky gully ((s)   ) and through a forest of majestic gum trees ((t)   ). We finally emerged to find ourselves standing on the edge of a plateau. Before us lay a magnificent freshwater lake, which would be an excellent place to establish the new settlement.

We have named the lake   (u)   . Our task now is to hurry back to   (j)   and convey the happy news to Admiral   (c)   .

Justin Case
Captain, Royal Marines

OXFORD UNIVERSITY PRESS

Proper nouns are special names for people, places or things. Proper nouns always begin with capital letters. For example: *Queen Elizabeth, Australia, Anzac Day, Mazda*

1 Read the imaginary account on page 8 from the diary of Captain Justin Case.

Write proper nouns of your choice so that the account makes sense.

For example: **(a)** might be *Tuesday*, **(c)** might be *Henderson*, **(j)** might be *Cosy Bay*

a _____   b _____   c _____

d _____   e _____   f _____

g _____   h _____   i _____

j _____   k _____   l _____

m _____   n _____   o _____

p _____   q _____   r _____

s _____   t _____   u _____

2 Use proper nouns to complete the following.

a   What is the name of the street, road, etc. on which you live? _____

b   What are the names of two of your friends? _____

c   Write a teacher's name. _____

d   Write the names of the months that have fewer than 31 days. _____

_____

e   Write the name of a mountain. _____

3   Match the common nouns in Box A with the proper nouns in Box B.

A

a   politician _____   b   explorers _____

c   city _____   d   author _____

e   book _____   f   river _____

g   road _____   h   sacred site _____

i   planet _____   j   aeroplane _____

k   sportsperson _____   l   company _____

B

Nile
Main Street
Uluru
Scott Morrison
The Hobbit
Microsoft
Beijing
Jupiter
Ash Barty
Boeing 747
William Shakespeare
Burke and Wills

CHALLENGE

On a separate piece of paper or on a computer, use each of the letters of the alphabet to begin the proper nouns for names of:

a   26 countries   b   26 girls' names   c   26 boys' names   d   26 animals.

(If you get stuck with x, use it anywhere in your proper noun.)

Marina's open night

* a project called *Our Heroes*
* sliced tomatoes
* 2 pianos
* 6 banjos
* bookshelves
* knives
* radios
* dictionaries
* a project on wolves
* live salmon and trout
* pet mice
* trousers with different kinds of stitches
* loaves of bread
* scissors
* stories

* sewing-needle boxes
* dolls' dresses
* autumn leaves
* street directories
* live goldfish
* Ari's project on butterflies
* models of teeth
* atlases of cities and countries
* Carla's project on monkeys
* Rema's project on mosquitoes
* a book called *Highways and Railways of Australia*
* videos of various class activities
* Anton's PowerPoint presentation on why wild dogs and dingoes are a threat to sheep and calves

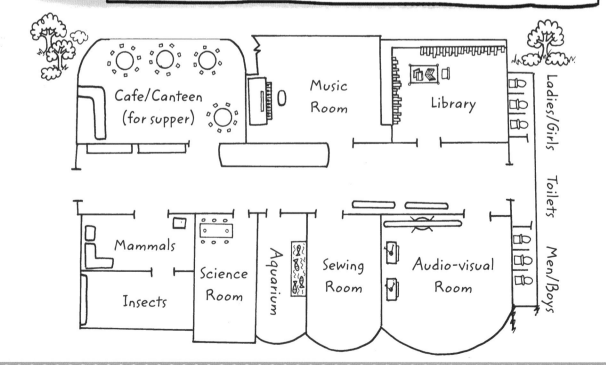

OXFORD UNIVERSITY PRESS

Do you remember these rules for plural nouns?

1   For many nouns, just add *s* to make plural nouns. For example: *girls, lamps, books*
2   For nouns ending in *ch, sh, ss* or *x*, add *es*. For example: *matches, bushes, foxes*
3   For nouns ending in *y*, change the *y* to *i* and then add *es*. For example: *cities, diaries*
4   For nouns ending in *y* following a vowel, just add *s*. For example: *boys, trays*
5   For most nouns ending in *f* or *fe*, change *f* or *fe* to *v* and then add *es*. For example: *halves, knives*
6   To form some noun plurals, there is a change in spelling. For example: *feet, children*
7   For nouns ending in *o*, add *es*. For example: *potatoes, heroes*
8   For most nouns from other languages, and for nouns ending in *o* that have been abbreviated, just add *s*. For example: *pianos, kimonos, radios*

1 Write the following nouns as **plurals**.

a   woman _____
b   calf _____
c   key _____

d   convoy _____
e   room _____
f   box _____

g   wolf _____
h   studio _____
i   pliers _____

j   shelf _____
k   Saturday _____
l   glass _____

m   echo _____
n   gas _____
o   volcano _____

p   x-ray _____
q   photo _____
r   banjo _____

s   foot _____
t   dictionary _____
u   life _____

v   ostrich _____
w   toy _____
x   wallaby _____

2 Change the following sentences to **plural**.

a   The frightened donkey hid in the ditch as the wolf and the elf tramped by. _____
_____

b   Marni took her scissors, shears and needle and, in a moment, she had created the most fantastic dress that the princess had ever seen. _____
_____

3 Write **plurals** from the box to match these clues.

spies   thieves   brooches   banjos   mosquitoes   aviaries   attorneys   cypresses

a   blood-sucking insects _____
b   lawyers _____
c   secret agents _____
d   musical instruments _____
e   jewellery _____
f   bird cages _____
g   trees _____
h   robbers _____

CHALLENGE

Look at page 10. Marina's school is holding an open night for parents. Marina has a box filled with things to display or use in the rooms and on the noticeboards. Help Marina get organised for the special night. On a separate piece of paper or on a computer, write or type the name of each item in the best location possible. For example: *live goldfish – in the aquarium, street directories – in the library*

The loaded dog

Dave Reagan, Jim Bently and Andy Page were sinking a shaft at Stony Creek in search of a rich gold quartz reef which was supposed to exist in the vicinity.

○   ○   ○

They had a big, black, young retriever dog — or rather an overgrown pup, a big, foolish, four-footed mate, who was always slobbering round them and lashing their legs with his heavy tail that swung round like a stockwhip. Most of his head was usually a red, idiotic, slobbering grin of appreciation of his own silliness. He seemed to take life, the world, his two-legged mates, and his own instinct as a huge joke. He'd retrieve anything; he carted back most of the camp rubbish that Andy threw away. They had a cat that died in hot weather, and Andy threw it a good distance away in the scrub; and early one morning the dog found the cat, after it had been dead a week or so, and carried it back to camp, and laid it just inside the tent flaps, where it could best make its presence known when the mates should rise and begin to sniff suspiciously in the sickly, smothering atmosphere of the summer sunrise.

He used to retrieve them when they went in swimming; he'd jump in after them, and take their hands in his mouth, and try to swim out with them, and scratch their naked bodies with his paws. They loved him for his good-heartedness and his foolishness, but when they wished to enjoy a swim they had to tie him up in camp.

by Henry Lawson

Adjectives are words that describe people, animals, places and things.
For example: The **adventurous** trio was sinking a **deep** shaft in search of a **quartz** reef.
                 Sometimes a writer adds more adjectives to sharpen the image for the reader.
                 For example: a **rich gold quartz** reef

1 Read the passage from 'The loaded dog'. Write eight adjectives that describe the men's dog.

_____

2 Write adjectives from the passage that describe the following.

    a   the dog's tail _____   **b**   a joke _____

    c   the dog's grin _____   **d**   the weather when the cat died _____

    e   the atmosphere _____

Adjectives are often used to compare things.
For example: a big retriever; a bigger retriever; the biggest retriever
                 a heavy tail; a heavier tail; the heaviest tail

3 Complete this table with suitable comparative adjectives.

large	larger	
fast		fastest
thick		
	naughtier	

Did you know that some common and proper nouns can be used as adjectives? For example: birthday cake, boat refugee, Pacific gull

Sometimes, instead of adding -er or -est when using comparative adjectives, we need to write *more* or *most* before them.
For example: The dog was foolish. His dog was more foolish, but my dog was the most foolish.

4 Use the adjectives in bold to compare three things.

    a   Sally was **excited**, Ella was _____ but

        Maddy was _____.

    b   Dave was **suspicious**, Jim was _____ but

        Andy was _____.

A simile is a figure of speech that uses adjectives to compare things.
For example: as slippery as an eel (*slippery* is the adjective)

5 Use adjectives from the box to complete these similes.

    a   as _____ as a cucumber

    b   as _____ as a lamb

    c   as _____ as a fox

    d   as _____ as an owl

gentle
cunning
wise
cool

CHALLENGE

A sprinkling of adjectives can enliven writing, but be careful not to overdo it. On a separate piece of paper or on a computer, use adjectives and interesting nouns to write or type a brief description of one of the following.   **a** a jungle scene   **b** a desert landscape   **c** a seashore on a stormy day

This looks like a job for...?

In downtown Pondsville, there is a raging fire in a tall skyscraper. Several people are trapped on the roof of the building.

With his sharp hearing, Tad Pole, mild-mannered reporter for the Daily Lilypad, hears the desperate cries.

Quickly Tad leaps into a nearby telephone box and shortly emerges as ...

DYNAMIC DUCK

?

Hang on — that's not right.

... and emerges as ...

SUPER SNAIL

?

Hang on — that's not right either.

... and emerges as ...

MIGHTY MOTH

?

Nope. Let's have another go.

... and emerges as ...

WONDER WORM

?

Wrong again!

... and emerges as ...

Editor's note: By the time our confused hero emerges as **FEARLESS FROG!!!**, the people on the building have been bravely rescued by our noble firefighters, the raging fire has been extinguished, the damaged building has been rebuilt, sold and knocked down by a developer and in its place a luxurious block of apartments has been erected!

An adjective tells us more about a noun. In sentences, an adjective usually comes before the noun it is describing. For example: *Tad Pole was a **mild-mannered** reporter. (reporter is a noun)*
*Our **confused** hero emerged from the **red telephone** box.*
***Several** people were trapped but that hero rescued them.*

1 Write the adjectives from the comic strip that are used in the names of the following.

a   the duck _____

b   the snail _____

c   the moth _____

d   the worm _____

e   the frog _____

2 Write adjectives from the comic strip that describe the following.

a   Tad Pole's hearing _____

b   the firefighters _____

c   our hero _____

d   the apartment block _____

e   the cries of the trapped people _____

f   the fire _____

g   the skyscraper _____

h   the building after the fire _____

i   Tad Pole, the reporter _____

Adjectives can have three degrees of comparison:
*   positive – when the adjective is in its simplest form: fast, ugly, dangerous
*   comparative – when the adjective compares two people, groups or things: faster, uglier, more dangerous
*   superlative – when the adjective compares more than two people, groups or things: fastest, ugliest, most dangerous

3 Underline the adjectives.

a   The valiant frog struggled desperately to get into his colourful costume.

b   On top of the smoke-filled building, the impatient people waited for their witless hero to arrive.

c   By the time the sluggish superhero had arrived on the scene, the razed building had been replaced by a grand apartment block.

Some adjectives compare. For example: *a **tall** building, a **taller** building, the **tallest** building*

4 Write adjectives of comparison in the gaps in these sentences. For example: *A hippopotamus is **larger** than a dog.*

a   The frog was brave, the people were braver, but the firefighters were _____.

b   Dynamic Duck's hearing is good, Super Snail's hearing is _____, but Tad Pole's hearing is _____.

c   The telephone box is luxurious, the old building was _____ luxurious, but the new apartment block is the _____.

CHALLENGE

On a separate piece of paper or on a computer, write or type three adjectives for each of the following.

a   Tad Pole / Fearless Frog   b   the people on the skyscraper   c   the firefighters

Foiled again!

Here are the main characters from the play 'Foiled again!'

The furious Queen Astrid of Migglewomp

The detestable Count Meout

The valiant Sam Flashygrin

The faithful dog Jellybean

The delightful Clover Uptomanees

The cowardly Sandy Myles

The hideous Erk

OXFORD UNIVERSITY PRESS

Adjectives are words that describe nouns.

For example: a **soft, furry** toy. Biffo was the **funniest** clown at the circus.

When adjectives or articles (a, the, an) are added to nouns, they form a noun group. Some adjectives can be formed by adding suffixes (endings) to nouns or verbs.

For example: Count Meout is **detestable** = detest (verb) + -able

Note: When adding endings to some words, the spelling of the base word must change before the ending is added.

1 a Use the suffixes in the box to change each noun or verb to an adjective.

> -able   -ous   -ful   -ate   -less   -ish   -ant   -ent   -ic   -ly

danger _____	honour _____	fame _____	cheer _____
glamour _____	use _____	fashion _____	villain _____
objection _____	help _____	fool _____	rely _____
innocence _____	energy _____	fury _____	thought _____
disgrace _____	courage _____	beauty _____	please _____
nerve _____	sheep _____	mind _____	consider _____
spite _____	monster _____	peace _____	faith _____
care _____	fiend _____	coward _____	marvel _____
self _____	chivalry _____	hero _____	grace _____
style _____	affection _____	friend _____	child _____
power _____	humour _____	fortune _____	agree _____
courtesy _____	ridicule _____	beast _____	colour _____

b On a separate piece of paper or on a computer, write noun groups by using the list of new adjectives you have written to expand the descriptions of the seven characters from the play 'Foiled again!'

For example: the cowardly, nervous but humorous Sandy Myles

CHALLENGE

How many adjectives can you form from the letters in the boxes below? You may use letters more than once.

> S   R   E   T   I   A   H   F   N   D   Y   U

How Phan Ku created the world

Over thousands of years, many cultures have sought to explain how the world came to be. These stories are called creation stories. The stories seem fanciful to modern people but when told so long ago, they seemed the best way to explain why things were the way they were. Here is a creation story from ancient China.

In the beginning, there was emptiness except for a single egg. Phan Ku was asleep inside that egg for thousands of years. Trapped with Phan Ku inside the egg was the energy Yin and Yang.

As Phan Ku slept, he grew and grew. Soon he was a massive giant and his tiny egg could no longer hold him. With a mighty blow Phan Ku smashed his egg open.

Phan Ku had escaped from his egg. Yin and Yang also escaped. Yin rose into the sky to become the brilliant light. Yang floated down and became the warm earth.

Phan Ku needed more space between Yin, the sky, and Yang, the earth. He stood with legs apart and took the sky upon his broad shoulders. He pushed and pushed and pushed. Each day he pushed more and each day the space between earth and sky grew wider.

While he pushed, Phan Ku used his mighty hammer and sharp chisel to carve out the world. For 18 000 years, the giant pushed and worked.

Sometimes Phan Ku was happy, which made the weather gentle and calm. Sometimes the giant was tired, lonely and upset. This would cause storms and wild weather to rage upon the new world.

After 18 000 years Phan Ku was old and weak. He decided that he had lived long enough. Phan Ku lay down and closed his eyes. His last breath became the swirling clouds and whistling wind. His

last words became the frightening thunder. The sun and the moon came from the final sparkle of his dying eyes. His arms and legs became the towering mountains. The giant's blood flowed from his body to form the rivers, lakes and seas. From Phan Ku's hair sprang the grass, the trees and all the flowers. From Phan Ku's final resting place industrious bugs emerged and these bugs eventually became all of the animals and people.

Phan Ku had created a wonderful new world from the cold, dark emptiness that had come before him.

1 Find and write **adjectives** from the story on page 18 that best describe these nouns.

a _____ giant   b _____ light

c _____ hammer   d _____ chisel

e _____ and _____ weather   f _____ shoulders

g _____ clouds   h _____ mountains

2 Find **proper nouns** in the story to match these descriptions.

a the person the story is about _____

b the country from where the story originally came _____

c the egg's energy _____ and _____

3 Find **adjectives** in the story that are **synonyms** (words with similar meanings) for these words.

a huge _____   b wide _____

c small _____   d weary _____

4 Add a **suffix** to each of the following adjectives to form **nouns**.

For example: cool + ness = coolness

a empty _____   b lonely _____

c happy _____   d gentle _____

5 Add a **suffix** to each of the following nouns to form **adjectives**.

a breath _____   b harm _____

c wonder _____   d fright _____

CHALLENGE

Use **adjectives** to complete these sentences.

a After 18 000 years Phan Ku had become _____ and _____ .

b Sometimes the giant was _____ , _____ and
_____ .

TOPIC 1: ASSESS YOUR GRAMMAR!

Nouns, adjectives and noun groups

1 Shade the bubble next to the **common noun**.

○ write   ○ door   ○ happily   ○ you

2 Shade the bubble next to the word that is not an **abstract noun**.

○ hatred   ○ lightning   ○ memory   ○ sadness

3 Shade the bubble next to the **collective noun** for **fish**.

○ school   ○ pack   ○ bunch   ○ crowd

4 Shade the bubble next to the word that is an **abstract noun**.

○ bravery   ○ foot   ○ egg   ○ homework

5 Shade the bubble below the **proper noun** in this sentence.

I would only get a game with the Bandits if I practised every day.

○   ○   ○   ○

6 Shade the bubble next to the correct **noun plural** for **dingo**.

○ dingos   ○ dingi   ○ dingoes   ○ dingies

7 Shade the bubble next to the correct **noun plural** for **goose**.

○ goose   ○ gooses   ○ goosies   ○ geese

8 Shade the bubble next to the **noun group** in this sentence.

We sailed quietly through the eerie fog.

○ sailed quietly   ○ quietly through   ○ through the   ○ the eerie fog

OXFORD UNIVERSITY PRESS

9 Shade the bubble next to the **adjective** that best describes an ocean.

○ succulent　　　○ turbulent　　　○ wholesome　　　○ athletic

10 Shade the bubble next to the **adjective** that best describes a villain.

○ heroic　　　○ delicate　　　○ evil　　　○ homely

11 Shade the bubble next to the **adjective** that completes the following:

quick, ⟨　　　　　　　　⟩ *, quickest*

○ quicker　　　○ quickly　　　○ quickening　　　○ quicks

12 Shade the bubble next to the **adjective** that completes the following:

bad, worse, ⟨　　　　　　　　⟩

○ baddest　　　○ worser　　　○ worsest　　　○ worst

13 Shade the bubble next to the **comparative adjective** that would best complete this sentence.

Of all the dogs, he was the ⟨　　　　　　　　⟩ *dog in the obedience class.*

○ smart　　　○ smarter　　　○ smartest　　　○ smarts

14 Shade the bubble next to the **comparative adjective** that would best complete this sentence.

I was good, he was ⟨　　　　　　　　⟩ *but she was by far the best.*

○ gooder　　　○ better　　　○ bestest　　　○ goodest

TICK THE BOXES IF YOU UNDERSTAND.

I understand the difference between common, proper, collective and abstract nouns. ☐

I understand that there are different rules for making nouns plural. ☐

Adjectives describe nouns. ☐

I understand the difference between positive, comparative and superlative adjectives. ☐

James and the Giant Peach

And now the peach had broken out of the garden and was over the edge of the hill, rolling and bouncing down the steep slope at a terrific pace. Faster and faster and faster it went, and the crowds of people who were climbing up the hill suddenly caught sight of this terrible monster plunging down upon them and they screamed and scattered to right and left as it went hurtling by.

At the bottom of the hill it charged across the road, knocked over a telegraph pole and flattened two parked cars as it went by.

Then it rushed madly across about twenty fields, breaking down all the fences and hedges in its path. It went right through the middle of a herd of fine Jersey cows, and then through a flock of sheep, and then through a paddock full of horses, and then through a yard full of pigs, and soon the whole countryside was a seething mass of panic-stricken animals stampeding in all directions.

The peach was still going at a tremendous speed with no sign of slowing down, and about a mile farther on it came to a village.

Down the main street of the village it rolled, with people leaping frantically out of its path right and left, and at the end of the street it went crashing right through the wall of an enormous building and out the other side, leaving two gaping round holes in the brickwork.

by Roald Dahl

OXFORD UNIVERSITY PRESS

Verbs tell us what is happening or being done. Talented authors, such as Roald Dahl, choose verbs carefully to create a sharper image for the audience. Look at the following example from the text on page 22. The author could have written: 'animals *going* in all directions'. Instead he wrote: 'animals *stampeding* in all directions'.

1 Read the extract from *James and the Giant Peach*. Circle the **verbs** that tell about the action of the peach.

A simple verb is usually one word that comes after the subject of the sentence.
For example: *The ball* **bounced**. *The children* **ran**. *James* **climbed** *the tree*.
Verbs answer questions such as: *What are you doing? What is it doing? What did they do? What will she do?*

2 Underline the simple verbs in these sentences.

a   The peach rolled down the steep slope.   b   The peach bounced down the steep slope.

c   Faster and faster and faster it went.   d   It charged across the road.

e   They screamed.   f   The peach flattened two parked cars.

g   It came to a village.   h   People leapt frantically out of its path.

A compound verb (verb group) can be two or more words that include a main verb and a helping verb.
(The helping verb can also be called an auxiliary verb. An auxiliary verb helps identify the tense of the verb.)
The ball **will bounce**. Here *bounce* is the main verb, *will* is the helping verb.
They **are running** *from the peach*. Here *running* is the main verb, *are* is the helping verb.

3 Underline the compound verbs (verb groups) in these sentences.

a   The peach had broken out of the garden.   b   Crowds of people were climbing up the hill.

c   The monster was plunging down upon them.   d   It went crashing right through the wall.

e   The peach went rolling down the steep slope. f   The peach was still going.

4 Write the compound verbs from these sentences and then circle the auxiliary (helping) verbs.

a   The workers were returning to the building site. _____

b   The animals were stampeding in all directions. _____

c   The peach had broken through the fence. _____

d   James was waiting in the garden. _____

e   Our basketball team is practising every day for the Grand Final. _____

CHALLENGE

On a separate piece of paper or on a computer, write or type interesting sentences of your own using each of the **simple verbs** shown below as a **compound verb** (verb group).

a   walk   b   fly   c   dance   d   bought   e   choose

The Trampers' Club

May 2020

The Trampers' Club Newsletter

Hi everyone and welcome to the May newsletter! It's mostly about rules this month, as the committee felt a few reminders might be in order.

First, some hiking rules …

Older members should always wear a white Trampers identity badge on hikes.

New members must wear their red Trampers identity badge on at least their first three hikes. This will certainly help our 'Hiking buddy' system work better.

Now some club rule reminders …

- Meetings will take place on the first Saturday of each month.
- Could members please remember to bring a plate of food or a drink to each meeting?
- All members must remove their footwear before entering the new clubhouse.
- All members should use the rear door to enter the clubhouse. (The committee might relax this rule once the barbecue area is completed.)

General news

Congratulations to Emma, Max, Geti and Leo on their great hike to Mt Prospect and back — well done guys. We ought to hold a viewing night soon.

Remember that the general hike to Walpurra Bay will take place on Sunday 25 June (weather permitting) — all are welcome!

Any current members who would like to introduce new members to the club may do so at any monthly meeting. (We would welcome any new members.)

Finally, members, their friends and families can donate to the club online. If you would like to make a donation, talk to Sam or Mish. Any donation will be gratefully received.

See you all on Saturday 20 May. Don't forget to bring your wet weather gear — it's winter, remember!

Samantha Cerano (Club President)

Some verbs tell the degree to which something might happen. They tell us the level of certainty or probability of something happening.

These verbs are called modal verbs or modal auxiliaries. They are helping verbs and must always be used with a main verb. The 10 most common modal verbs are: *can, could, may, might, shall, should, will, would, must, ought to.*

1 Read the text on page 24, then underline the modal verbs in these sentences. Remember, modal verbs can be more than one word.

a Meetings will take place on the first Saturday of the month.

b All members should use the rear door to enter the clubhouse.

c Members can donate to the club online.

d We ought to hold a viewing night soon.

e Older members should always wear a white Trampers identity badge on hikes.

f This will certainly help our 'Hiking Buddy' system work better.

g All members must remove their footwear before entering the new clubhouse.

2 Circle the modal auxiliary that correctly completes each of the following.

a Will / Shall you turn off the television?   b May / Can you ride a bicycle?

c Should / Shall they come back later?   d May / Will you open your books please?

3 Use a modal auxiliary from the information box at the top of the page to complete each sentence.

a _____ I please go to the toilet?

b _____ a fruit bat see in the dark?

c If I had the time I _____ play tennis with you.

d If you are not ready _____ I come back when you are?

CHALLENGE

Write four more rules for the Trampers' Club. Include a modal verb in each rule.

_____

_____

_____

_____

The amazing Verbo

The Amazing Verbo is standing.

The Amazing Verbo is waiting.

The drum is rolling.

The Amazing Verbo is growing tense.

The Flying Finns are jumping.

The time has come.

The Flying Finns are touching down.

The Amazing Verbo is flying.

The Amazing Verbo is soaring.

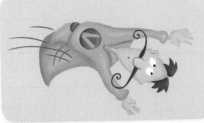

The Amazing Verbo is landing…

…badly.

Verbs can tell us when something has happened. Verbs tell us whether the action in a sentence is in the past, present or future. We call this verb tense.

For example: *I walked.* (past) *I am walking.* (present) *I will walk.* (future)

The bird flew. (past) *The bird is flying.* (present) *The bird will fly.* (future)

1 Write if these sentences are in the past, present or future tense.

a   The Flying Finns are jumping. _____

b   The time will come. _____

c   Yesterday I swam 12 lengths of the pool. _____

d   Now is the time to ask questions. _____

e   The cat crept slowly towards the bird. _____

f   On my sixteenth birthday I will be getting a motorbike. _____

2 Circle the correct past tense verb in each sentence.

a   Tezza has (broke/broken) another window with that cricket shot.

b   A burglar who forced the door open has (stole/stolen) the jewels.

c   I (saw/seen) what was happening.

3 Complete this verb tense table.

Verb	Past	Present	Future
write	have written or wrote	am writing or writes	will write
wear	_____ or wore	_____ or wears	_____
know	have known or _____	_____	_____
_____	have drunk or _____	are drinking or _____	_____
sing	have sung or_____	_____ or _____	_____

4 Change the following sentences to the past tense.

For example: *On the camp we **will swim** for one hour every morning.*

*On the camp we **swam** for one hour every morning.*

a   I am flying to Brisbane tomorrow. _____

b   The farmer's paddock is full of corn. _____

c   Gerri is drinking her milk. _____

CHALLENGE

The story of the amazing Verbo on page 26 is written in the present tense. On a separate piece of paper or on a computer, rewrite the story twice: once in the past tense and then again in the future tense.

There's something fishy going on

All fish are aquatic vertebrates, meaning they have a backbone and live in water. According to experts, there are approximately 24 000 species of fish in the world. Fish are an important source of food worldwide.

Oysters are marine molluscs. Oysters are unusual because they can be male one year and female the next!

Jellyfish have tentacles. The tentacles of the lion's mane jellyfish can reach up to 60 metres from its body. That's the length of two basketball courts. The collective noun for jellyfish is a **smack**.

The glassfish is completely transparent. All of its bones and organs can be clearly seen.

The largest fish of all is the whale shark, which can grow up to 15 metres long.

The electric eel is a freshwater predator. It has electric organs, which it uses to stun its prey. The electric eel can deliver a 500-volt shock. The usual power of a home's electricity supply is 240 volts!

Barracuda are saltwater fish. When hungry, a barracuda will hunt for a whole school of fish. When it has eaten its fill, the barracuda herds the remaining live fish into shallow water. It then keeps them prisoner by guarding them until it is ready to eat again at its leisure.

Some fish are actually known to get seasick!

Verbs can be doing verbs (*walked, ran, climbed*, etc.), saying verbs (*said, called, asked*, etc.), thinking verbs (*decide, consider, believe*, etc.), feeling verbs (*like, love, hate, wish*, etc.) or relating verbs (*am, is, are, was, were, has, have, had*). We often use relating verbs in the timeless present tense when we are stating facts such as the facts about fish on page 28. Timeless present tense is used to indicate actions that are always happening. Here are some examples of the timeless present tense: *All fish **are** aquatic vertebrates. Fish **live** in water. All fish **have** backbones.*

1 Underline the **timeless present tense verbs** in these sentences.

a The whale shark is the largest fish of all.

b Jellyfish live in smacks.

c The glassfish is completely transparent.

d Fish are an important source of food worldwide.

e Jellyfish have tentacles.

2 Write timeless present tense verbs from the box to complete these sentences.

> eat   live   is   have   are

a Barracuda _____ saltwater fish.

b Omnivorous animals _____ plants and meat.

c Fish _____ scales.

d An oyster _____ a marine mollusc.

e All fish _____ in water.

> *Use timeless present tense when:*
> - *the action is general*
> - *the action happens all the time*
> - *the statement is always true.*

CHALLENGE

Write four or five facts about an animal that you know something about. Make sure your facts are written in **timeless present tense**.

_____

_____

_____

_____

_____

_____

It's Adverb Man!

More powerfully built than a locomotive!**

**a toy locomotive, that is — or at least the package it comes in and as long as the package is paper, not plastic, because plastic's pretty tough these days.

Able to bravely enter buildings through a single door!*

*as long as it's not locked.

Moves faster!***

***when threatened with a speeding bullet.

Able to catch trains!****

****on time.

Uses his heat vision helpfully to conquer evils of the world!*****

*****especially when there's a power failure and Mrs Man wants a hot cuppa.

Master of invisibility******

******particularly when it's time to do the dishes.

Are you in trouble? Being held for ransom? Trapped upstairs in a burning building? Perhaps you're currently falling out of an aeroplane over the Pacific Ocean. Then for all your superdeeds you definitely need **ADVERB MAN**: a superhero for the new millennium.

Contact Adverb Man. CALL NOW!

You can always reach him on this toll-free number:

37488199999210023813125 (only $80 per minute).

Kids, ask your parents first.

OXFORD UNIVERSITY PRESS

Adverbs usually add meaning to verbs. They can tell us **how**, **when**, **where** and **how often**.
For example: *She walked quickly.* (How? *quickly*) *Let's go in now.* (When? *now*)
Put your boots there. (Where? *there*) *I have seen that film twice.* (How often? *twice*)

1 Read 'It's Adverb Man!' on page 30 and then write whether the adverbs underlined below tell how, when, where or how often.

a bravely enter _____

b can always reach _____

c call now _____

d trapped upstairs _____

2 Underline the adverbs in these sentences and write whether they are telling how, when, where or how often.

a The mouse crept quietly into the room. _____

b I think the rain will stop later. _____

c The motorbike skidded sideways. _____

d He never swims alone. _____

Sometimes adverbs can be used to compare.
For example: *Mickey fought* **bravely**, *Jeda fought* **more bravely** *but Rona fought* **most bravely**.
When comparing, most adverbs that end with -ly use *more* and *most*.
When comparing, most single-syllable adverbs add -er and -est.
Exception: When using *early* as an adverb, treat it the same as single-syllable adverbs (add -er and -est).

3 Use the above rules to help you complete this table of adverbs that compare.

Positive	Comparative	Superlative
bravely	more bravely	most bravely
powerfully	_____	_____
helpfully	_____	_____
fast	_____	_____
late	_____	_____
early	_____	_____

Modal adverbs can be used with verbs to add a degree of certainty or possibility. For example: **Perhaps** *you forgot to pack your socks. It seemed* **likely** *he would miss the train. You* **obviously** *spent some of your pocket money. Perhaps, likely and obviously are modal adverbs because they modify or tell us more about what is possible or certain. Modal adverbs can be more than one word. For example: in fact, no doubt*

4 Circle the modal adverbs and underline the verbs they modify.

a His argument certainly convinced me.

b We absolutely loved the house.

c Jet Black definitely won the race.

d The bus is probably running late.

CHALLENGE

Reread the advertisement for Adverb Man on page 30. Then, on a separate piece of paper or on a computer, create an advertisement for a new 'wonder product' that can give the consumer incredible powers. In your ad, include as many adverbs as you can to help sell your product. For example: *superbly, powerfully, certainly, better, best, quickly, fast, loudly, really, surely*

The golden apples

Atalanta was not only beautiful, she could also run faster than any mortal.

Because Atalanta had been raised in the forest by the bears, her hunting skills were extraordinary and she could run more swiftly than the fastest deer.

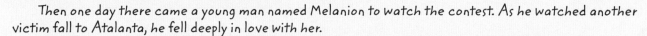

Atalanta was very eager to find a husband but she was advised by the gods that if she married, a terrible disaster would befall her.

Atalanta's father desperately wanted to see his daughter married, and many young men sought Atalanta's hand in marriage. Upon her father's pleading, Atalanta agreed to marry on the condition that her suitors run a foot race with her. Any suitor who defeated her could take her for his wife, but those who were beaten would be put to death. Time after time, many unfortunate suitors died brutally after losing a race to Atalanta — for no one could run more quickly than the cruel beauty.

Then one day there came a young man named Melanion to watch the contest. As he watched another victim fall to Atalanta, he fell deeply in love with her.

"I must win this beauty for myself," he thought, "but how can she be my wife? Surely I cannot run faster than she."

Melanion eagerly sought the advice of Aphrodite, the goddess of love, who had always considered Melanion one of her favourite mortals. She agreed to help and gave the youth three golden apples, saying, "Use these wisely and the one you love shall be yours."

Melanion gratefully took the apples and set about challenging Atalanta to a race.

The huntress was taken aback by the handsome young man and wished that he did not have to die. However, her fear of a possible disaster forced her to reluctantly accept Melanion's challenge.

The race began and for a while Atalanta ran alongside Melanion, gazing wistfully at the attractive youth. With a sigh she began to slowly pull away from him. Melanion took a golden apple from his tunic and lobbed it out in front of Atalanta. She stopped suddenly, picked up the apple, and stared at it with wonder.

Melanion took the lead, but unfortunately it did not last for long. Soon the huntress had caught up to him and was about to pass him when he threw a second apple in front of her. Again Atalanta stopped to admire the enchanting fruit. With lungs on fire, Melanion surged once more to the lead. He could see the winning post not far ahead.

Atalanta soon made up the ground that she had lost and Melanion once more struggled to keep up. He took the final apple from his tunic and tossed it off to the side of the track. Atalanta could not resist stopping to pick up the third apple. Melanion realised that this was his last chance.

Although his throat was parched and his lungs felt ready to explode, he lunged desperately for the finish line. Atalanta realised now that she had been tricked. She sprinted furiously after the young man. But she had left her final dash too late! To the cheers of the crowd, Melanion crossed the finish line seconds before Atalanta.

Without hesitation he claimed Atalanta for his bride. Although she was saddened by defeat, Atalanta accepted her fate graciously and became Melanion's wife.

NB: Atalanta's fears about a disaster were later realised when an angry Zeus (the chief god) turned both Atalanta and Melanion into lions after they had accidentally misused one of Zeus's temples.

Adverbs usually tell us more about verbs.
Adverbs that tell us how are called adverbs of **manner**.
For example: *Atalanta ran quickly.* (How? *quickly*)
Adverbs that tell us when are called adverbs of **time**.
For example: *Melanion raced Atalanta yesterday.* (When? *yesterday*)
Adverbs that tell us how often are called adverbs of **number**.
For example: *The young men only had the chance to race once.* (How often? *once*)
Adverbs that tell us to what degree are called adverbs of **degree**.
For example: *Atalanta almost won the last race.* (What degree? *almost*)

1 Read 'The golden apples' then underline the adverbs in the following sentences and write the type of adverb. For example: *He fell deeply in love with the huntress.* (manner or degree)

a Many unfortunate suitors had died brutally. _____

b Atalanta gazed wistfully at Melanion. _____

c Soon the huntress had caught up to him. _____

d Atalanta realised now that she had been tricked. _____

e Again Atalanta stopped to admire the enchanting fruit. _____

Like some adjectives, some adverbs also compare.
For example: I hit **hard**, he hits **harder** but she hits **hardest**.
         The suitors ran **swiftly**. Melanion ran **more swiftly** but Atalanta ran the **most swiftly** of all.

2 Complete this table of adverbs that compare.

Positive	Comparative	Superlative
swiftly	more swiftly	most swiftly
hard	harder	hardest
silently	more silently	
		most bravely
quickly		
wisely		

When we expand around a main adverb to add detail, this is sometimes called an adverb group.
For example: *more swiftly, extremely swiftly, so swiftly*

3 Use the adverb group *more swiftly* in a sentence of your own.

_____

_____

CHALLENGE

On a separate piece of paper or on a computer, make a list of all of the adverbs you can find in 'The golden apples'. When you have finished, compare your list with your classmates.

Tom Swifties

Come on through to my surgery.

Don't these lollies cost anything?

I'll change the globe for you.

What are you painting?

I think winter's nearly with us.

I took my raft over the river's rough water.

How far is it across the Nullarbor?

I like to sleep all the time when we go camping.

I wonder if the concrete's set yet.

What should I wear to my wedding?

Isn't that bag too heavy for me to lift?

Wouldn't you prefer a poodle?

You gave me two less than a dozen!

Oh no! Why didn't you water my plants while I was away?

What do we do after the high jump?

Next you move your counter up the ladder or down the snake.

I wonder when we'll be able to launch the boat.

I can see clearly through this window now.

Would you like me to get something for you?

I'm off to race in the Melbourne Cup.

OXFORD UNIVERSITY PRESS

Adverbs tell us more about verbs. Tom Swifties are a form of humorous word play. The words spoken by Tom Swift, an adventure hero, would be followed by an adverb that had something to do with what he had said. For example: *"I'm in bed with the measles,"* said Tom **infectiously**. (The word 'infectiously' is an adverb meaning spreading germs or disease.)

1 Using the speech bubbles opposite, write what each of these 'Tom Swifties' said.

a _____ asked Tom artfully.

b _____ said Tom, the builder, firmly.

c _____ said Tom, the cleaner, transparently.

d _____ said Tom tensely.

e _____ said Tam, the jockey, hoarsely.

f _____ said Tom intently.

g _____ asked Tom, the labourer, weakly.

h _____ thought Tom, the sailor, tidily.

i _____ said Tom, the adventurer, rapidly.

j _____ said Tom, the electrician, lightly.

k _____ asked Tom freely.

l _____ asked Tom eventually.

m _____ said Tom gamely.

n _____ asked Tom, the bridegroom, suitably.

o _____ asked Tom plainly.

p _____ asked Tom witheringly.

q _____ asked Tom doggedly.

r _____ said Dr Tom patiently.

s _____ asked Tom, the waiter, fetchingly.

t _____ said Tom, the weather forecaster, coldly.

Adverbs sometimes tell us more about adjectives. They are often used to downplay or add emphasis to an adjective. For example: *Tom Swifties are* **very** *funny.* (The adverb intensifies the adjective *funny.*)
Tom Swifties are **somewhat** *funny.* (The adverb tones down the adjective *funny.*)

2 Circle the adverb used to add emphasis to or to downplay each underlined adjective.

a   I am extremely upset I won't see you.

b   He was very unhappy.

c   I am really sorry I missed you.

d   She looked simply uninterested.

CHALLENGE

On a separate piece of paper or on your computer, make up your own Tom Swifties using the adverbs below.

a   fashionably   b   wickedly   c   colourfully   d   clearly

Mixed-up proverbs

When you read the proverbs below, you will notice that they have become jumbled. (See exercises on page 37.)

Birds in the hand flock together.

Never look a gift horse while the iron is hot.

A bird in glass houses is worth two before they're hatched.

Rome wasn't built over spilt milk.

Don't count your chickens in the bush.

People of a feather shouldn't throw stones.

Make hay until you come to it.

Don't cry in one basket.

Don't cross the bridge in a day.

Don't put all your eggs in the mouth.

Charity begins while the sun shines.

Strike at home.

OXFORD UNIVERSITY PRESS

A phrase is a group of words without a verb. A phrase sometimes does the work of an adjective to provide a fuller description. For example: *The girl **with red hair** ...*   *The shop **around the corner** ...*
Prepositional phrases begin with prepositions such as *with, on, in, under, near, about, over, of, into, around,* etc.

1 The proverbs on page 36 are jumbled. Unjumble them and write them on a separate piece of paper, in your workbook or on a computer, so that they make sense. Now add **prepositional phrases** to complete these proverbs.

a   Birds _____ stick together.

b   People _____ should not throw stones.

c   A bird _____ is worth two _____.

2 Write the prepositional phrases from the box that best fit the characters below. Write roman numerals to match.

> i   in a glamorous ball gown   ii   in oil-stained overalls   iii   with sore feet
> iv   with a deep voice   v   with perfect balance   vi   in a camouflaged uniform
> vii with a weathered face   viii with violin in hand

a   the opera singer _____   b   the bushwalkers _____

c   the acrobats _____   d   the soldier _____

e   the movie star _____   f   the mechanic _____

g   the farmer _____   h   the musician _____

Prepositional phrases can also do the work of an adverb to tell **when**, **where** or **how** an action takes place.
For example: *She arrived **at six o'clock**.* (tells when she arrived)
                     *The bus stopped **by the school gate**.* (tells where the bus stopped)
                     *The doctors worked **with great skill**.* (tells how the doctors worked)

3 Underline the prepositional phrase from each sentence and write whether it is telling **when**, **where** or **how**.

a   The exchange teacher comes from Brazil. _____

b   The herd of elephants lumbered across the plain. _____

c   Our school concert will begin at 7 o'clock. _____

d   The waves crashed onto the rocks with a loud roar. _____

CHALLENGE

Write the phrases from the unscrambled proverbs that best tell us more about these words.

a   built _____   b   cry _____

c   put (eggs) _____   d   don't look (a gift horse)_____

The games we played

Below are five recollections by elderly people about the games they played when they were your age. Do you recognise any of the games? Remember that when these people were young, there were no computer games or electronic devices.

1 "We couldn't afford to buy a footy so we would get an old newspaper and fold it and make a package until it was about six inches long and a couple of inches wide. We would tie a string around the middle of it. Of course it wouldn't bounce and it was so hard that when you kicked it, it sometimes hurt your foot."

2 "You got five sheep's knucklebones from the local butcher and you got mum to boil them until they were clean. Once clean, they were Jacks to be tossed and caught on your hand. If you wanted them to be fancy, you could get your paint box out and paint them in pretty colours."

3 "You could make your own corrugated iron canoe. There was always plenty of old iron lying around. You had to bend your sheet of iron down the middle and work it and smash it until it was the right shape. You could then prise a bit of tar off the edge of the road, melt it down in a billy can and pour it over the end of your canoe to seal it. They were fun to make but they usually sank like stones as soon as you launched them."

4 "Aggies were the best to have. They were clear with a spot of colour coming from the centre. Connies were coloured glass. Some of us had Cat's eyes, which were rare and valued. Clayies or clay dabs were made of baked clay and we called them Commonohs. It was a good trick to get hold of a Steelie (which was a ball-bearing). It would break all the others in games like Big Ring, Little Ring or Threes."

5 "You could play humming gum-bubbles. You got new gum leaves in the spring and peeled off the fine, rubbery skin. When you sucked and blew, like bubblegum, it would give off a loud pop."

OXFORD UNIVERSITY PRESS

1 Find verbs in the recollections on page 38 that match the following definitions.

    a   force by levering _____

    b   hit with the foot _____

    c   heat liquid until it bubbles _____

    d   drawn in by the mouth _____

    e   heat a solid until it becomes a liquid _____

2 Write the past tense of these verbs. For example: swim – swam

    a   sink _____

    b   blow _____

    c   catch _____

    d   make _____

    e   toss _____

    f   hurt _____

    g   get _____

    h   call _____

3 Underline or circle the adverbs in these sentences.

    a   Mum slowly boiled the sheep's knucklebones in a pot on the stove.

    b   When you blew it, it popped loudly.

    c   They were fun to make but they usually sank like a stone.

4 Add prepositional phrases to complete these sentences.

    a   We would tie a string _____.

    b   You could prise a bit of tar _____.

    c   You got new gum leaves _____.

    d   We got Mum to boil them _____.

    e   They were clear with a spot of colour coming _____.

CHALLENGE

Complete this table of comparative adverbs.

hard	harder	_____
well	_____	best
little	less	_____
_____	nearer	nearest
early	_____	earliest

TOPIC 2: ASSESS YOUR GRAMMAR!

Verbs, adverbs and prepositional phrases

1 Shade the bubble below the **verb** in this sentence.

Several cars crashed on the busy freeway.

○   ○   ○ ○

2 Shade the bubble below the **simple verb** in this sentence.

The snake slithered silently towards the unsuspecting mouse.

○   ○   ○   ○

3 Shade the bubble next to the **compound verb** (verb group) in this sentence.

The passengers were waiting impatiently for the late train.

○ the passengers   ○ were waiting

○ waiting impatiently   ○ late train

4 Shade the bubble below the **auxiliary verb** in this sentence.

Police are looking for a man with a scar across his left cheek.

○ ○   ○   ○

5 Shade the bubble next to the **past tense verb** that completes this group, and then write the verb in the box.

```
┌─────────────────────────────────┐
│                                 │
└─────────────────────────────────┘, is buying, will buy
```

○ buys   ○ buyed   ○ bought   ○ am buying

6 Shade the bubble below the **modal verb** in this sentence.

Fans should enter the stadium through the east gate.

○   ○   ○   ○

7 Shade the bubble next to the word that is **not** a modal verb.

○ might   ○ would   ○ will   ○ run

OXFORD UNIVERSITY PRESS

8 Shade the bubble next to the correct sentence.

○ Mitch has broken the light on his new bicycle.

○ Mitch has broke the light on his new bicycle.

○ Mitch has breaked the light on his new bicycle.

○ Mitch has broked the light on his new bicycle.

9 Shade the bubble that shows the following sentence written in the past tense.

During our English class we will write a story about a fearsome dragon.

○ During our English class we are writing a story about a fearsome dragon.

○ During our English class we writted a story about a fearsome dragon.

○ During our English class we wrote a story about a fearsome dragon.

○ During our English class we was writing a story about a fearsome dragon.

10 Shade the bubble below the adverb in this sentence.

The superhero used his powerfully built body to lift the stricken locomotive.

ㅣ ㅣ ㅣ ㅣ
○ ○ ○ ○

11 Shade the bubble next to the prepositional phrase in this sentence.

Captain Spack Jarrow manoeuvred the boat alongside the jetty.

○ Captain Spack Jarrow   ○ manoeuvred the boat

○ on the boat   ○ alongside the jetty

TICK THE BOXES IF YOU UNDERSTAND.

Verbs tell us what is happening in a sentence. ☐

Auxiliary verbs are helping verbs used with a main verb. ☐

Modal verbs tell how sure we are about taking an action. ☐

Adverbs add meaning to verbs telling when, where or how something happened. ☐

Prepositional phrases are small groups of words beginning with a preposition that add details about when, where, how and why. ☐

UNIT 3.1 Text cohesion – antonyms, synonyms and homonyms

The fabulous Nym Brothers

Presenting those fabulous proponents of acrobatic dexterity …

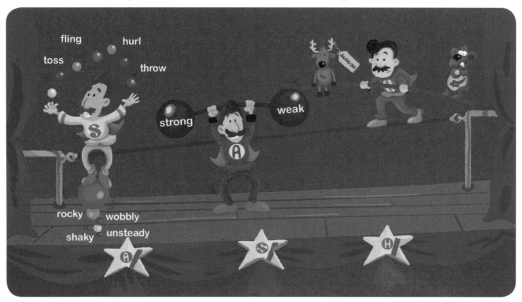

What the critics said …

about Syno Nym   Fantastic, wonderful, marvellous, amazing,
extraordinary, astonishing, incredible, stupendous!
Without a thesaurus what more can I say?

Theo Sawrus (Sydney Mourning Harold)

about Anto Nym   Sometimes he's good and sometimes he's bad.
Sometimes he's happy but sometimes he's sad.
He rises to the ceiling then falls to the floor.
You'll be wishing for less rather than more.

Oppy Zit (Melbourne Sunburn)

about Hommy Nym   A dear deer? Yes we saw that! A bare bear?
Yes we saw that too!

But what we really wanted to see was Hommy taking a trip on his trip across the
tightrope. An acrobat all at sea — now that would have been something to see.

Pete Peat (The Weekly Prophet — a non-profit magazine)

OXFORD UNIVERSITY PRESS

Writers often repeat key words or replace them with synonyms or antonyms to add interest or compare and contrast a character's features.

Antonyms are opposites.
For example: *asleep/awake* *modern/ancient*

Synonyms are words with similar meanings.
For example: *big, large, huge, gigantic*

1 Match the words in the box with their antonyms.

> strong   less   minor   down   idle   departure   rough   conclude

a up _____ **b** begin _____ **c** busy _____

d major _____ **e** weak _____ **f** arrival _____

g more _____ **h** smooth _____

Sometimes prefixes can be added to words to make antonyms.

2 Add the prefixes un-, dis-, mis-, in- or im- to form antonyms.

a behaviour _____ **b** activity _____

c accurate _____ **d** possible _____

e complete _____ **f** honest _____

g necessary _____ **h** usual _____

Sometimes suffixes can be changed to form antonyms. For example: *hopeful/hopeless*

3 Change the suffix of each word so that it becomes an antonym.

a careful _____ **b** useless _____ **c** cheerful _____

d merciful _____ **e** joyless _____ **f** pitiless _____

4 Circle the word that does not belong in each group of synonyms.

a fantastic   wonderful   marvellous   ordinary   amazing

b wobbly   shaky   steady   rocky   unsteady

c toss   throw   catch   fling   hurl

d strong   weak   powerful   mighty   sturdy

e halt   cease   stop   commence   conclude

Homonyms can be homophones or homographs.
Homophones are words that sound the same but have different meanings.
For example: blew, blue; wait, weight
Homographs are words that are spelt the same but have different meanings.
For example: bow = ribbon, bow = front of a ship; bow = to bend at the waist, bow = a weapon for shooting arrows

CHALLENGE

Write homophones and their meanings. For example: *dear = expensive* and *deer = a large mammal*

a boy = a young male AND _____

b creek = a small stream AND _____

c flower = a plant blossom AND _____

A sting in the tail

The hobbit, Bilbo Baggins, has mysteriously lost his dwarf companions during the night. He finds himself alone in the silence and complete darkness.

That was one of his most miserable moments. But he soon made up his mind that it was no good trying to do anything till day came with some little light, and quite useless to go blundering about tiring himself out with no hope of any breakfast to revive him. So he sat himself down with his back to a tree, and not for the last time fell to thinking of his far-distant hobbit-hole with its beautiful pantries. He was deep in thoughts of bacon and eggs and toast and butter when he felt something touch him. Something like a strong sticky string was against his left hand, and when he tried to move he found that his legs were already wrapped in the same stuff, so that when he got up he fell over.

Then the great spider, who had been busy tying him up while he dozed, came from behind him and came at him. He could only see the thing's eyes, but he could feel its hairy legs as it struggled to wind its abominable threads round and round him. It was lucky that he had come to his senses in time. Soon he would not have been able to move at all. As it was, he had a desperate fight before he got free. He beat the creature off with his hands — it was trying to poison him to keep him quiet, as small spiders do to flies — until he remembered his sword and drew it out. Then the spider jumped back, and he had time to cut his legs loose. After that it was his turn to attack. The spider evidently was not used to things that carried such stings at their sides, or it would have hurried away quicker. Bilbo came at it before it could disappear and stuck it with his sword right in the eyes. Then it went mad and leaped and danced and flung out its legs in horrible jerks, until he killed it with another stroke; and then he fell down and remembered nothing more for a long while.

There was the usual dim grey light of the forest-day about him when he came to his senses. The spider lay dead beside him, and his sword-blade was stained black. Somehow the killing of the giant spider, all alone by himself in the dark without the help of the wizard or the dwarves or of anyone else, made a great difference to Mr Baggins. He felt a different person, and much fiercer and bolder in spite of an empty stomach, as he wiped his sword on the grass and put it back into its sheath. "I will give you a name," he said to it, "and I shall call you Sting."

from *The Hobbit* by J. R. R. Tolkien, reprinted by permission of HarperCollins Publishers Ltd © 1975

OXFORD UNIVERSITY PRESS

When writing, it is often necessary to omit or replace words to keep the text interesting.
For example: *Tina ate two bananas and Simon ate three bananas* would be better written as *Tina ate two bananas and Simon ate three.*
Another way a writer might keep text interesting for the reader is to repeat key words or replace them with pronouns or synonyms.
For example: *Bilbo was alone and miserable. The hobbit sat down and he pondered what he could do.*
In these sentences, *Bilbo* and *the hobbit* are interchangeable, while *he* is a pronoun replacing *Bilbo* and *the hobbit.*

1 Read 'A sting in the tail' on page 44, then rewrite the following sentences omitting or replacing words, where necessary, to make the sentences easier to read.

   a   Bilbo took out his sword. He killed the spider with the sword.

   _____

   b   A strong sticky string was against his left hand. He found that his legs were bound with the strong sticky string. _____

   _____

   c   He beat the creature off with his hands. The creature was trying to poison him.

   _____

2 Write the word that has been omitted or replaced by the word in **bold**.

   a   Bilbo dreamed of the delicious berries he had eaten that morning. Then he remembered he had **some** in his pocket. _____

   b   "I have a powerful sword. Would you like **one**?" he said. _____

3 Underline the words in the sentences below that have been used to replace the bold words.

   a   Sitting on the embankment was **a gnome**. The little fellow was wearing a yellow cap upon his head. In his left hand the odd chap held the lost map.

   b   **The grapes** hung in bunches from the vines. The fruit looked tender and juicy and we couldn't wait to pick and taste the delightful delicacies.

   c   **Billy** strode into the garden. He was carrying **baby Gerty** on his shoulders and she had a huge grin across her face.

   d   I can't find **my umbrella**. Have you seen it?

   e   Congratulations to **Chloe**, **Evie and Tan**. They achieved top marks in the spelling test. Well done guys!

CHALLENGE

In the text opposite, underline words that replace or refer to the main character. Use a different colour for each word replaced.
For example: *The* **hobbit, Bilbo Baggins**, *has mysteriously lost his dwarf companions during the night. He finds himself alone in the silence and complete darkness.*

Ivan goes for gold

It's the final night of weightlifting here at the Olympics. Heavyweight lifter Ivan de Golmeddle prepares for his final attempt. A successful lift for Ivan will mean GOLD! GOLD! GOLD!

Ivan approaches the barbell.

He bends and grasps the bar.

The photographers prepare themselves, for they are sure he will break the world record, which has stood for 20 years.

Ivan begins his lift.

He struggles.

He strains.

He puffs and pants.

But no world record or gold medal for Ivan today. However, we do believe that the photographers were very happy with their photos.

OXFORD UNIVERSITY PRESS

Pronouns or possessives can be used to replace or refer to a noun mentioned earlier in a sentence or text. Possessives answer the question: *Who owns it?* Possessives can include *my, your, his, her, its, our* and *their*. For example: *The dog gnawed at **its** bone.* Who owns the bone? *The dog.*

1 Rewrite the sentences. Replace the repeated noun with a suitable pronoun or possessive.

a Ivan begins Ivan's lift. _____

b The photographers were very happy with the photographers' photos.

_____

c Ivan struggles. Ivan strains. Ivan puffs and Ivan pants.

_____

First person pronouns are: *I, me, we, us, mine, ours.* They refer to those speaking (*me* or *us*). For example:
I have piano lessons on Wednesdays after school.
When **we** travelled to Mildura for a holiday **we** took **our** pets with **us**.

> *Personal pronouns refer to people or things: I, me, we, us, you, he, him, she, her, it, they, them*
> *Possessives refer to ownership: mine, ours, yours, his, hers, theirs*

2 Use the first person pronouns and possessives to complete this description of the weightlifting contest written by Ivan de Golmeddle.

_____ approached the barbell. _____ bent _____ knees and grasped the bar which lay in front of _____. _____ began to lift but _____ struggles were in vain. Unfortunately, the gold medal would not be _____ this year.

Second person pronouns are: *you* and *yours.* They refer to those spoken to (*you*).
For example: *Did **you** bring your homework today? Is that baseball bat **yours**?*

3 Change these sentences from first person to second person pronouns.

For example: *I was late for school. You were late for school.*

a I went on a holiday. _____

b Bree's room is much tidier than mine. _____

Third person pronouns are: *he, him, his, she, her, hers, it, its, they, them, theirs.* They refer to those spoken about (*him, her, it* or *them*). For example: **He** will wear **his** raincoat while **he** waits for **them** to arrive.

4 Rewrite the sentences in the third person.

a Last year I competed in my first Olympic Games. _____

_____

b You couldn't lift your bar above your head. _____

_____

CHALLENGE

In question 2, writing in the first person as Ivan de Golmeddle, you wrote about the weightlifting competition. On a separate piece of paper or on a computer, complete the description from the photographers' point of view. Your description will be in the first person.

Did you hear about...?

a

Did you hear about the skeleton that was attacked by a dog which ran off with some bones?

He didn't have a leg to stand on!

b

Did you hear about the man who made a hot dog stand by stealing its chair?

c

Did you hear about the jellybean that went to school to become a Smartie?

d

Did you hear about the restless medical student who couldn't become a doctor?

He didn't have the patients!

e

Did you hear about the one-handed man who was arrested trying to cross the road against the traffic lights?

He was on his way to the secondhand shop!

f

Did you hear about the wooden car that had wooden wheels and a wooden engine?

It wooden go!

g

Did you hear about my best friend who was sat on by an elephant?

Now he's my flatmate!

h

Did you hear about the tree whose leaves blushed every time they saw the nature strip?

OXFORD UNIVERSITY PRESS

Who, **which**, **whose**, **whom** and **that** are relative pronouns. Relative pronouns can stand in the place of a noun and can join two sentences.

For example: *Did you hear about the jellybean **that** went to school to become a Smartie?*

Did you hear about the jellybean? The jellybean went to school to become a Smartie.

1 Write the relative pronoun (or pronouns) from each joke on page 48.

a _____   b _____

c _____   d _____

e _____   f _____

g _____   h _____

2 Use a relative pronoun to join these sentences.

a Amanda turned 12 on Friday. Amanda is having a party on Saturday. _____

_____

b This is the house. It was built by Mr and Mrs Rasheed. _____

_____

c The athlete could not compete. Her ankle was injured. _____

_____

d She is a reliable person. I can trust her. _____

_____

Who refers only to people. For example: *Carrie, **who** is the school captain, thanked the visitors on our behalf.*
Which refers to animals, plants and things. For example: *The cat, **which** crossed the busy freeway, used up eight of its nine lives.* That refers to people, animals, plants and things.

3 Write endings following the relative pronouns to complete these sentences.

a The soldier who _____

b The old oak tree, which _____

c The lady that _____

4 Which noun has been replaced by a relative pronoun? Circle it.

For example: *The footballer **who** broke his leg was out of action for 10 weeks.* ((footballer) leg weeks)

a I met a boy called Anthony **whose** mother drives a truck. (boy mother truck)

b On the tractor is the farmer **who** killed the deadly snake. (tractor farmer snake)

c The bank was robbed by a criminal **that** wore a gorilla mask.
(bank criminal mask)

CHALLENGE

On a separate piece of paper or on a computer, write or type your own sentences containing these relative pronouns: who   which   whose   that

Why the Moon waxes and wanes

Myths and legends were used by cultures in the past to explain why things are the way they are. Here is a legend from the Iroquoian people of North America to explain, in their beliefs, why the Moon changes its shape during the course of a month.

Once, according to legend, the Sun and the Moon were husband and wife. They lived together side by side, travelling across the sky. Each day they would reach the hole at the edge of the sky, and the Sun, being the more important, would pass through, followed by the Moon.

One day, the Moon quarrelled with the Sun. She pushed through the hole at the edge of the sky before her husband. This action enraged the Sun. He scolded his wife, the Moon, and sent her away to the dark world below.

Great Turtle, the master of all animals, heard of the argument between the Sun and the Moon. He set off to search for the Moon and eventually found her pining away. She had lost most of her light and was so thin that instead of a ball she was merely a tiny crescent.

The Great Turtle spent much time with the Moon. He coaxed and cajoled and mended her broken heart and set her on her own course again. Gradually she became her own round self once more and she travelled across the sky in search of her husband.

However, the Sun refused to recognise his wife and as she approached he turned away from her. The Moon began to pine away again.

And so the cycle continues to this day. The Moon grows bright and radiant with hope, only to be ignored by her husband. Slowly she pines away, shrinking with sorrow as she follows the unforgiving Sun across the sky.

adapted from an Iroquoian legend

OXFORD UNIVERSITY PRESS

Paragraphs are used to organise information into logical sections so that the text is more easily understood. Paragraphs usually contain a number of sentences about one particular point. A topic sentence often begins a paragraph. It introduces or summarises the main point of the paragraph.

The *first paragraph* in a text body is often an introductory paragraph. It introduces us to what the text is about. The *final paragraph* in a text body is usually a concluding paragraph. It sums up what the text has been about. The *first word of a paragraph* is usually indented or written further in from the margin than the rest of the paragraph.

1 Read 'Why the Moon waxes and wanes' on page 50, then answer the questions below about the paragraphs and topic sentences in the story.

a   How many paragraphs does the story on page 50 have? _____

b   Write the first sentence of the introductory paragraph. _____

_____

c   Write the first sentence of the concluding paragraph. _____

_____

d   How many sentences are there in the fourth paragraph? _____

e   Which paragraph introduces the Great Turtle? _____

f   Which paragraph tells us how the Sun reacted to the Moon's rudeness? _____

g   Write the topic sentence the author has used in the third paragraph. _____

_____

Text connectives help to link text together. They give the reader signs about what is likely to come in the text.

2 Copy the six text connectives that the author has used in the story on page 50.

_____

_____

CHALLENGE

On a separate piece of paper or on a computer, write or type five to 10 paragraphs about one of the topics below. Remember to include an introductory paragraph and a concluding paragraph. Your paragraphs can be any length. Begin each paragraphs with a topic sentence and, wherever possible, use text connectives of your own or from the box.

- Your own explanation of why the Moon waxes and wanes
- A report about some recent sports results
- How the echidna got her spines
- My hobby
- Explain how to care for a pet (of your choice)
- Why the tiger has stripes
- The best day of my life so far
- Skateboards, bikes, skates and scooters!
- My typical day
- How the mountains and rivers were formed

> **Text connectives:**   for example, in other words, therefore, so, then, next, afterwards, soon, finally, later, firstly, also, furthermore, otherwise, however, besides, even so, despite this, though

Simmo and Lee's team of the century

Sports broadcasters Simmo and Lee have finally decided on the six players that make up their TEAM OF THE CENTURY.

Fullback: Orson Carte

Simmo says... Orson is as old as the hills but he's as safe as a bank in defence. He's as strong as an ox, as hard as nails and as cool as a cucumber in a crisis. Attacks find it difficult to get past him because he is like a rock on that fullback line.

Orson Carte

Halfbacks: Amanda Lynne and Owen Ulotts

Lee says... Young Mandy is as brave as a lion and as swift as an arrow. She is as light as a feather and moves like a ballerina, but don't let that fool you for she can be as tough as old boots too.

My choice for the other halfback is Owen Ulotts, who can run like the wind and go through packs like a steam train.

Amanda Lynne

Centre: Bootsun Hall

Simmo says ... You can't really go past the veteran Bootsun in this position. Built like a tank, as fit as a fiddle, as graceful as a swan and always as busy as a bee. What more could you ask?

Owen Ulotts

Forwards: Willy Kickett and Rhoda Tramm

Lee says... Willy moves like a cat. He's as sly as a fox and has the eye of a hawk.

Simmo says... Rhoda will be a good back-up for Willy. She is as agile as a monkey, she attacks the ball like a demon and then strikes like lightning — I think she'll have a top game.

Bootsun Hall

Here's what **Coach Tom Artow** had to say about his team: This team is like a machine — they're like clockwork. When they train they are as keen as mustard and, come game day, I think, as a unit, they'll be as sharp as a tack. I'll be as proud as a peacock if they win on Saturday.

Simmo's tip for Saturday: The Team of the Century by 100 points or I'm as silly as a sausage.

Willy Kickett

Lee's tip for Saturday: The Team of the Century by 50 points or I'm as foolish as a court jester.

Rhoda Tramm

A simile is used to compare one thing with another. A simile tells us that something is *like* something else. Similes begin with *like* or *as*.

For example: The moon was **like** a grapefruit.
The water of the lake was **as** clear as crystal.

1 Write two similes that have been used to describe each character.

a Orson Carte _____

b Amanda Lynne _____

c Bootsun Hall _____

d Willy Kickett _____

e Rhonda Tramm _____

> Remember: You can make your writing more lively by using similes. But don't overdo it in the way that Simmo and Lee have done on page 52!

2 Write the names of the characters who have been compared using similes.

a a steam train's power _____   b a swan's grace _____

c an ox's strength _____   d a monkey's agility _____

e a peacock's pride _____   f an arrow's speed _____

g a hawk's vision _____   h a jester's silliness _____

3 Complete the following similes using words from the box.

a as wise as an _____   b as fresh as a _____

c as bald as an _____   d as blind as a _____

e as ugly as _____   f as flat as a _____

g as light as a _____   h as gentle as _____

i as sick as a _____   j as warm as _____

k as slippery as an _____   l as quiet as a _____

> toast
> eel
> sin
> owl
> egg
> daisy
> pancake
> mouse
> feather
> bat
> dog
> lamb

4 Use words from the box to complete these similes.

a Snow covered the ground like a _____.

b He was as _____ as a kitten.

c The fleece on Mary's lamb was as white as _____.

d The hallway was as dark as a _____.

e The children were rewarded for being as good as _____.

f Before her concert performance, Mamie's legs were like _____.

> playful, blanket, gold, jelly, dungeon, snow

CHALLENGE

On a separate piece of paper or on a computer, make up your own similes by completing the following.

a as ... as silk   b her knees were like ...   c as nervous as ...   d as pretty as ...

e he ran like ...   f it sank like ...   g as sharp as ...   h he crashed like ...

Meet a metaphor

Rod was forced to eat his words.

Cassie is full of beans today.

Mark Diswright was over the moon with his test results.

Jenny is the apple of her Granny's eye.

Myra's legs were jelly at the sight of the huge audience.

It was raining cats and dogs.

OXFORD UNIVERSITY PRESS

We use metaphors to make our writing more colourful. Like a simile (see Unit 3.6), a metaphor is a word picture. It compares something or someone to something as if it is that thing.

For example: *the night was a cloak*
                    she played second fiddle
                    the Moon was a grapefruit

1 Match the **metaphors** on page 54 with their meanings below.

a very happy and excited _____

b lots of energy _____

c regret what has been said _____

d to be adored by someone _____

e raining very heavily _____

f in a very nervous state _____

> A simile compares one thing to another: *He ate like a pig.* A metaphor uses words to say that two things are the same: *He was a pig at dinner.*

2 Underline and then write your own explanations for the **metaphors** used in the sentences below.

a During the search for the missing children, he was a tower of strength to the family.

_____

b When it comes to the garden, Aunty Em certainly has green fingers. _____

_____

c A way to recycle old tyres? Now there's food for thought. _____

_____

d Poor Tim has another broken heart. _____

e During the closing stages of the game, Terri was a tiger in the packs. _____

_____

f "We will leave no stone unturned in our search for the culprits," said Sergeant Clark.

_____

CHALLENGE

On a separate piece of paper or on a computer, explain what you think these **metaphors** mean.

a Her blood froze.   b He waited with his heart in his mouth.

c She is a live wire.   d They were down in the dumps.   e His blood boiled.

Celebrations

Eid ul-Fitr

During the holy month of Ramadan, those of Muslim faith do not eat or drink between sunrise and sunset. Fasting during Ramadan demonstrates to Muslims that the good things in life should not be taken for granted. It is also a reminder that the poor and destitute of the world suffer from constant hunger.

Eid ul-Fitr celebrates the end of the Ramadan fasting period. The word *eid ul-fitr* is an Arabic word which means 'breaking the fast'. For three days Muslims celebrate a joyous festival of feasting, visiting loved ones and exchanging gifts.

Trung Thu

Trung Thu is a Vietnamese celebration held on the fifteenth day of the eighth lunar month. The festival celebrates the beauty of the moon. During the Trung Thu, families gather together and children are spoilt with treats and tasty moon cakes, which are traditional sweet-filled cakes. Children will often wear colourful masks and carry glowing lanterns, which represent the moon, out into the streets.

Hannukah

Hannukah is a Jewish festival – a festival of lights. It is celebrated for eight days, throughout which a candle on a *menorah* (candelabra) is lit each evening. During Hannukah, children receive a small present each evening. Special food such as *latkes* (potato cakes) are eaten during Hannukah.

Holi

Holi is a springtime Hindu festival celebrated in March by Hindus around the world. Holi coincides with the harvesting of wheat in India. On the evening before Holi, people light large bonfires to drive away evil spirits. On the following morning, people cover themselves with coloured powders and then squirt water over each other, covering themselves in a colourful mess. Children love Holi because it is a time when they are allowed to be as messy as they like.

Chinese New Year

Chinese New Year is one of the world's most colourful celebrations. Chinese New Year begins on the first day of the Chinese calendar, which is usually in February. The festival lasts for fifteen days and it is said that good luck, happiness and wealth for the new year will come to those who celebrate during this time. It is a time for feasting, colourful processions and family get-togethers. On New Year's morning children are given 'lucky' money in red envelopes.

1 Find antonyms in the text on page 56 for these words.

a sunrise _____

b rich _____

c ugliness _____

d good _____

e tidy _____

f sadness _____

2 Draw lines to match the words in Box A with their synonyms in Box B.

A

sunset

poor

celebrate

traditional

joyous

colourful

B

needy

vibrant

dusk

happy

commemorate

customary

3 Draw a circle around the correct homonyms in theses sentences.

a We sometimes **need/knead** to be reminded that **their/there** are **poor/pour** people in our world.

b **Your/You're allowed/aloud** to be messy during the celebration of Holi.

c **Its/It's** Trung Thu so **its/it's** time for delicious **sweet/suite** treats.

4 Complete these sentences using possessive pronouns to fill the gaps.

a Ravi covered _____ face with coloured powder and then began squirting _____ friends with water.

b "_____ mask is made of card," said Minh, "but _____ is made of crepe paper."

c Isabel's mother brought out _____ latkes and placed them in the middle of _____ table.

CHALLENGE

Complete these similes and metaphors.

a as quick as _____

b as hungry as _____

c as strong as _____

d as happy as _____

e the moon was a _____

f the waves crashed to the shore like _____

TOPIC 3: ASSESS YOUR GRAMMAR!

Text cohesion and language devices

1 Shade the bubble next to the antonym for **busy**.

○ idle　　　　　○ busily　　　　　○ unbusy　　　　　○ business

2 Shade the bubble next to a synonym for **dreadful**.

○ dreadless　　　　○ wonderful　　　　○ awful　　　　○ pleasant

3 Shade the bubble next to a prefix that could be used to make **patient** an antonym.

○ im-　　　　　○ un-　　　　　○ in-　　　　　○ mis-

4 Shade the bubble next to a suffix that could be used to change **merciful** to an antonym.

○ -tion　　　　　○ -less　　　　　○ -able　　　　　○ -ment

5 Shade the bubble next to the word that would correctly complete this sentence.

The travellers waited with ⬭ *bags inside the airport terminal.*

○ there　　　　　○ their　　　　　○ they　　　　　○ they're

6 Shade the bubble that shows which point of view the following sentence is written in.

I waited patiently until it was my turn and then I started my performance.

○ first person　　　○ second person　　　○ third person　　　○ fourth person

7 Shade the bubble that shows which point of view the following sentence is written in.

Later today they will arrive on their bikes at the rendezvous point.

○ first person　　　○ second person　　　○ third person　　　○ fourth person

8 Shade the bubble next to the **possessive** that would complete this sentence.

Marvin put on _____ slippers and relaxed in _____

favourite chair.

○ he   ○ him   ○ he's   ○ his

9 Shade the bubble below the **relative pronoun** in this sentence.

The man, who limped badly, struggled to get off the tram.

○   ○   ○   ○

10 Shade the bubble below the **text connective** in these sentences.

Preheat your oven to 180°. Next, prepare your vegetables.

○   ○   ○   ○

11 Shade the bubble next to the word that would best complete this **simile**.

As straight as an _____

○ highway   ○ barrel   ○ egg   ○ arrow

12 Underline the three **metaphors** that have been used in this verse from a well-known poem.

The wind was a torrent of darkness among the gusty trees,

The moon was a ghostly galleon tossed upon cloudy seas.

The road was a ribbon of moonlight over the purple moor,

And the highwayman came riding up to the old inn door.

TICK THE BOXES IF YOU UNDERSTAND.

Antonyms are opposites. ☐

Synonyms are words with similar meanings. ☐

Homonyms are words that look or sound the same. ☐

Possessive pronouns refer to ownership. ☐

Relative pronouns such as _who, which, whose, whom_ and _that_ can stand in the place of a noun OR join two sentences. ☐

Similes and metaphors are language devices that make our writing more descriptive and entertaining. ☐

UNIT 4.1 — Simple sentences – one main clause

I beg your pardon!

1 The politician was being cooked on the stove.

2 Mum had long hairy legs.

3 The smelly sock outsmarted the farmer.

4 The spider could see the dirt behind my ears.

5 My little brother was elected Prime Minister.

6 A huge red jelly was thrown into the washing machine.

7 The monster tickled the dog's belly.

8 The fox wobbled about on my plate.

9 My breakfast gobbled up the dwarves.

Simple sentences are made up of one main clause that can usually be divided into two parts:

a what is being talked about in the sentence (the **subject**) and

b what the rest of the sentence says about it (the **predicate**). The predicate always begins with a **verb**.

For example: *The cat meowed for its milk.* What is being talked about? *The cat* (subject)

What are we saying about it? That it *meowed for its milk.* (predicate)

1 On page 60, the subjects and predicates have been mismatched to make silly sentences. Rewrite the sentences correctly and then underline the **subject** in red and the **verb** that introduces the **predicate** in blue or black.

a _____

b _____

c _____

d _____

e _____

f _____

g _____

h _____

i _____

2 Underline the **subject** in each of these sentences.

a The audience clapped enthusiastically.

b The acrobat flipped casually over the barrel.

c Everyone at the party had a really great time.

3 Underline the **predicates** in these sentences.

a The jockey fell heavily.

b Our neighbour won the lottery.

c Smidge barked loudly at the intruder.

> The subject and verb in a clause or simple sentence must be in agreement.

4 Circle the correct **verb** that agrees with the underlined **subject**.

a We (go/goes) to the movies every month.

b The silly sentences (was/were) quite funny.

CHALLENGE

On a separate piece of paper or on a computer, use the mixed-up sentences and predicates on page 60 to write four of your own silly **sentences**. Make sure the **subject** and **verb** are in **agreement**.

For example: *The smelly sock was elected Prime Minister.*

You might also like to illustrate your sentences.

Transport quiz

SUBJECTS

Spacecrafts

Container ships

A tanker

Ferries

Locomotives

A Formula One car

Catamarans

A cruise ship

Hovercrafts

A prime mover

A skidoo

A turbojet

Tandems

VERBS AND OBJECTS

transports oil or
other liquids

flies long distances
carrying passengers

sail on two or more
hulls

use air cushions on
land or water

transport people, cars
and trucks

tow freight cars

races around tracks

hauls a trailer

slides across snow

carry containers

fly into space

carry two people

carries people on
ocean-going leisure
trips

OXFORD UNIVERSITY PRESS

The subject and verb of a sentence must agree in number. If the subject is singular, then the verb must be singular. For example: *The box **is** empty.* If the subject is plural then the verb must also be plural. For example: *The boxes **are** empty.*

1 Complete the transport quiz opposite by adding the **subjects** to the correct verbs and objects.

For example: *Container ships carry containers.*

a   A tanker _____

b   Locomotives_____

c   Ferries _____

d   A Formula One car _____

e   A turbojet _____

f   A skidoo _____

g   Spacecrafts _____

h   Catamarans _____

i   A cruise ship _____

j   Hovercrafts _____

k   Tandems _____

l   A prime mover _____

When **collective nouns**, money, lengths, weights and time are the **subject** of a sentence, they always take a singular verb in order to agree. For example: *A flock of birds **is** in the treetops.*

2 Circle the **verb** that **agrees** with the subject.

a   Seventy-five cents (was/were) all that she had left.

b   My team (is/are) winning by three goals.

c   The crowd (surge/surges) forwards.

Words such as *everybody, anybody, nobody, each, either* and *neither* always take a singular verb in order to agree. For example: *Either Mick or Sally **is** to blame.   Everybody **was** waiting for Mr Toms to arrive.*

Some words that end in *s* are really singular. For example: Measles is causing havoc at the school.

3 Circle the **verb** that **agrees** with the subject.

a   Everybody (was/were) wearing sunhats.

b   Neither of the sisters (are/is) at school today.

c   Each suspect (was/were) thoroughly searched by the police at the airport.

CHALLENGE

Write the **verb** *is* or *are* following these **subjects**.

a   the choir   b   the pair of trousers   c   the police   d   the cattle   e   the crew

_____   _____   _____   _____   _____

Whacky sentences

Subjects

The Prime Minister...

The wombat...

The weird alien...

My teacher...

The scary monster...

The hairy puppy...

The farmer...

The children...

Verbs

...met...

...ate...

...attacked...

...taught...

...chased...

...licked...

...milked...

...loved...

Objects

...the Queen...

...a soggy pickle sandwich...

...the prickly cactus...

...the littlies...

...my irritating brother...

...a plate of smelly cream...

...a green spotted cow...

...the funny clown...

Phrases

...at the Grand Prix

...on the rubbish tip

...in the desert

...every Monday morning

...in front of the shed

...under the table

...in the back paddock

...with the baggy pants

On page 64 you can see different sentence parts that make up a main clause. The subject tells us who or what the sentence is mainly about. The verb tells us what action the subject is carrying out. The object is the part of the sentence that is having something done to it. Phrases add details about where, when, how or why. For example: My teacher   teaches   the littlies   every Monday morning.

                 subject   **verb**   **object**   **phrase**

1 If you read each part of the sentences on page 64 in the order in which they are written, they will make sense. However, if you mix and match the different parts of the sentences, they will become very interesting. Write six new sentences by mixing the sentence parts.

For example: *The Prime Minister attacked a soggy pickle sandwich in front of the shed.*

_____

_____

_____

_____

_____

_____

2 Write the subjects in these simple sentences (main clauses).

a   The dog barked at the stranger with the dark glasses. _____

b   The old woman stirred the pot while chanting softly. _____

c   Jeda Jones threw a stick at the thieving crows. _____

3 Write the objects in these simple sentences (main clauses).

a   Mr Lu carried Simon to the waiting ambulance. _____

b   The pirates found their treasure under the tree on a deserted island. _____

c   Julius Caesar commanded a legion in Ancient Rome. _____

4 Underline the phrases in these simple sentences (main clauses).

a   He chased me from the ship.

b   The horse pulled the cart over the bridge.

c   On the starboard side of the ship the sailors raised the anchor.

5 Write the nine verbs that have been used in the sentences in Questions 2, 3 and 4.

_____

_____

CHALLENGE

On a separate piece of paper or on a computer, write or type one sentence about each of the topics listed below, making sure that each sentence contains a subject, a verb, an object and a phrase.

a   a passage of play in a game   b   a description of a wintry day   c   your favourite day of the week

Mongoose

He was a mongoose, rather like a little cat in his fur and his tail, but quite like a weasel in his head and his habits. His eyes and the end of his restless nose were pink; he could scratch himself anywhere he pleased, with any leg, front or back, that he chose to use; he could fluff up his tail till it looked like a bottle-brush, and his war-cry, as he scuttled through the long grass, was: "Rikk-tikk-tikki-tikki-tchk!"

One day, a high summer flood washed him out of the burrow where he lived with his father and mother, and carried him down a roadside ditch. He found a little wisp of grass floating there, and clung to it till he lost his senses. When he revived, he was lying in the hot sun on the middle of a garden path, very draggled indeed, and a small boy was saying: "Here's a dead mongoose. Let's have a funeral."

"No," said his mother; "let's take him in and dry him. Perhaps he isn't really dead."

They took him into the house, and a big man picked him up between his finger and thumb, and said he was not dead but half choked; so they wrapped him in cotton-wool, and warmed him, and he opened his eyes and sneezed.

"Now," said the big man (he was an Englishman who had just moved into the bungalow); "don't frighten him, and we'll see what he'll do."

It is the hardest thing in the world to frighten a mongoose, because he is eaten up from nose to tail with curiosity. The motto of all the mongoose family is, "Run and find out," and Rikki-tikki was a true mongoose. He looked at the cotton-wool, decided that it was not good to eat, ran all round the table, sat up and put his fur in order, scratched himself, and jumped on the small boy's shoulder.

"Don't be frightened, Teddy," said his father. "That's his way of making friends."

"Ouch! He's tickling under my chin," said Teddy.

Rikki-tikki looked down between the boy's collar and neck, snuffed at his ear, and climbed down to the floor, where he sat rubbing his nose.

"Good gracious," said Teddy's mother, "and that's a wild creature! I suppose he's so tame because we've been kind to him."

"All mongooses are like that," said her husband. "If Teddy doesn't pick him up by the tail, or try to put him in a cage, he'll run in and out of the house all day long. Let's give him something to eat."

from Rikki-Tikki-Tavi by Rudyard Kipling

OXFORD UNIVERSITY PRESS

Coordinating conjunctions are joining words used mainly to join two main clauses or simple sentences of equal importance. The main coordinating conjunctions are *and, but, so* and *or*.

For example: *He sat up **and** put his fur in order.*

               (*and* joins the equally important sentences *He sat up.* and *He put his fur in order.*)

Coordinating conjunctions can also be used to join two matching language features.

For example: *The mongoose's fur **and** tail were like a cat's.* (*and* joins the nouns *fur* and *tail*)

               *A high summer flood washed him out of the burrow **and** down a roadside ditch.*

               (*and* joins the phrases *out of the burrow* and *down a roadside ditch*)

1 Use the clues to help you underline the **coordinating conjunctions** in each sentence.

   a   He could scratch himself with any leg, front or back. (*I connect two adjectives.*)

   b   Rikki ran around the table and onto the boy's shoulder. (*I connect phrases.*)

   c   The mongoose lived with his mother and father. (*I connect two nouns.*)

   d   Rikki was a little like a cat in his fur and his tail but he was like a weasel in his head and habits. (*I connect two noun groups. I connect two main clauses. I connect two nouns.*)

Subordinating conjunctions join main clauses with subordinate clauses. Some common subordinate conjunctions are *because, if, after, although, until/till, since, where, when, while* and *as*.

Subordinate clauses start with a subordinate conjunction and cannot stand alone.

For example, the subordinate clause *because Jane rang the bell* needs a main clause before it can be used.

        *The children assembled at the classroom door **because Jane rang the bell**.*

               main clause   subordinate clause (dependent clause)

2 Circle the **subordinating conjunctions**, then write the **subordinate clauses**.

   a   It is the hardest thing in the world to frighten a mongoose because he is eaten up from nose to tail with curiosity. _____

   b   Rikki was a true mongoose although he looked like a cross between a cat and a weasel.

       _____

   c   A high summer flood washed him out of the burrow where he lived with his mother and father.

       _____

   d   He could fluff up his tail till it looked like a bottle-brush. _____

       _____

   e   Rikki-tikki climbed down to the floor where he sat rubbing his nose.

       _____

   f   If Teddy doesn't pick him up, he'll run in and out of the house all day long.

       _____

CHALLENGE

On a separate piece of paper or on a computer, write as many sentences as you can by using a different **conjunction** in the blank space of the following sentence.

We took refuge in the hut _____ *the wintry weather closed in.*

The wind and the frogs

Aboriginal Creation stories explain why things are the way they are. The following story is said to explain why frogs are afraid of the wind.

Long ago, the frogs were camped beside a waterhole. They were tending their campfire and preparing their evening meal when they heard the rustling of leaves and saw the reeds beside the water swaying in a gentle breeze.

What seemed to be a whispering voice asked the frogs if they would share their food and the warmth of their fire. The frogs looked nervously about but could see no one. They reluctantly agreed to the request for fear that if they refused, their invisible guest might harm them.

The frogs stayed awake all night, fearful of the stranger. As the sun rose, the leaves rustled gently, the reeds swayed back and forth and the same whispering voice seemed to say, "I will be back soon."

The frogs spent the day frightened about what was to become of them when the stranger returned. At midday, as the frogs sat nervously beside the waterhole, they saw a whirlwind rapidly approaching from the west. Soon the wind entered the frogs' campsite. It smashed the makeshift shelters that the frogs had built and it scattered the embers of their fire in all directions.

All the while, the same whispering voice seemed to call to the frogs to not be afraid. But the frogs were very afraid and they leapt into the waterhole for safety until the wind had passed.

To this day the frogs still react in the same way to even the slightest breeze in the reeds, for they fear the monster that comes with the wind has returned once more to destroy them.

OXFORD UNIVERSITY PRESS

A clause is a group of words that contains a verb. Main clauses can stand on their own as simple sentences. For example: *They grew fearful.* Subordinate clauses can be added to form complex sentences. For example: *They grew fearful **when the reeds began to sway***.

1 Read 'The wind and the frogs' on page 68. Use the coordinating conjunction *and* to join each pair of main clauses as one compound sentence, then find and underline the sentence in the extract.

a As the sun rose, the leaves rustled gently, the reeds swayed back and forth. The same whispering voice seemed to say, "I will be back soon."

_____

_____

_____

b It smashed the makeshift shelters that the frogs had built. It scattered the embers of their fire in all directions.

_____

_____

A subordinate clause:
- *always starts with a subordinating conjunction*
- *is not as important as the main clause in a sentence*
- *cannot stand alone as a sentence*
- *can be placed at the start, in the middle or at the end of a sentence.*

2 Join the main clauses in Box A to the subordinate clauses in Box B to form complex sentences.

A	B
The frogs looked nervously about	until the wind had passed
The frogs were tending their campfire	but could see no one
They leapt into the water hole for safety	when they heard the rustling of leaves

a _____

_____

b _____

_____

c _____

_____

3 Underline the subordinate clauses in these complex sentences.

a This is the building where the old woman lived.

b We decided to make camp because a thunderstorm was approaching rapidly.

4 Add your own main clause to each subordinate clause below to form complex sentences.

a _____ when the alarm rang.

b _____ because he had broken both paddles.

CHALLENGE

On a separate piece of paper or on a computer, add your own subordinate clauses to these main clauses. **a** We ran for the cover of the trees ... **b** ... we lost the game.

Fabulous monsters 1

The Cyclops

The Cyclops (*say* **sye**-*klops*) were a hideous race of one-eyed giants.

They are usually portrayed as lawless, man-eating shepherds, although they had once helped the gods to forge fabulous armour and weapons. They had been responsible for supplying the chief god, Zeus, with his most fearsome weapons — lightning bolts and thunder.

One Cyclops, named Polyphemus, and a son of the sea god, Poseidon, trapped the hero Odysseus (*say oh*-**dee**-*see-us*) and his crew inside his cave using a huge boulder to block the entrance.

The monster then began eating the unfortunate men until Odysseus used trickery to outsmart him. The hero told Polyphemus that his name was Nobody. He used the giant's wine to get him in a drunken stupor and then, with the help of his crew, he sharpened a large wooden stake and used it to blind Polyphemus.

In furious pain, Polyphemus called out to his fellow Cyclops that Nobody had blinded him. The Cyclops, believing Polyphemus to be drunk, ignored his cries. Odysseus and his men strapped themselves to the giant's huge sheep. When Polyphemus removed the boulder from the cave entrance to allow the sheep out to pasture, the heroes managed to escape.

Scylla and Charybdis

Scylla (*say* **sill**-*a*) and Charybdis (*say kar*-**rib**-*dis*) were sister sea-monsters.

Scylla had 12 legs and six heads on long necks and the mouths on each head contained three sets of terrible teeth. Some reports say that she also had several savage howling and snapping dogs' heads attached to her waist. She lived inside a cave on the high cliffs above a narrow channel. She would stretch out as ships passed to seize and devour the helpless crew members.

As if this was not enough for sailors to fear, on the other side of the channel, lying in wait should ships try to steer clear of Scylla, was Charybdis.

Charybdis was an unusual monster in that she was never seen or described, because she lay below the sea's surface. As unsuspecting ships passed close by, she created a fantastic and deadly whirlpool which sucked whole ships down. Once the crews had been drowned, Charybdis spat them out in a huge watery spray.

Because the channel was so narrow, avoiding Charybdis usually meant sailing within reach of her dreadful sister Scylla.

OXFORD UNIVERSITY PRESS

A simple sentence contains one main clause and therefore only one verb. For example: *The monster* **opened** *its deadly eyes*. A compound sentence contains two or more main clauses and therefore two or more verbs. For example: *The monster* **awoke** *and the hero* **approached**. A complex sentence contains a main clause and one or more subordinate clauses and therefore two or more verbs. For example: *The monster* **awoke** *and* **opened** *its deadly eyes as the hero* **approached**.

1 Make **compound sentences** by joining the sentences with **and**, **but** or **so**.

   a Scylla lived on the cliffs. Charybdis lived in the sea. _____

   _____

   b Polyphemus had trapped the crew. They used trickery to escape. _____

   _____

   c The ships tried to steer clear of the whirlpool. The channel was too narrow. _____

   _____

Here is a way to distinguish between types of sentences:
A simple sentence has only one verb. A compound sentence uses the coordinating conjunctions *and, but, so* and *or* to join two or more main clauses.
A complex sentence uses a subordinate conjunction to join a subordinate clause to a main clause.

2 Make **complex sentences** by joining the sentences using one of the conjunctions in the box.

   although, because, until, before, which, when

   a The Cyclops howled with pain. He had been blinded.

   _____

   _____

   b Odysseus and his men were amazed. A one-eyed giant appeared.

   _____

   _____

   c Cyclops are usually portrayed as lawless, man-eating shepherds. They had once helped the gods to forge fabulous armour and weapons.

   _____

   _____

3 Circle any subordinating conjunctions and write whether the following sentences are simple, compound or complex.

   a The Cyclops were a hideous race of one-eyed giants. _____

   b The monster began eating the unfortunate men until Odysseus used trickery to outsmart him. _____

   c Scylla had 12 legs and 6 heads on long necks and the mouths on each head contained 3 sets of terrible teeth. _____

   d The heroes managed to escape when Polyphemus removed the boulder from the cave entrance. _____

CHALLENGE

On a separate piece of paper or on a computer, write or type a simple sentence, a compound sentence and a complex sentence on a subject of your choice.

Bunyip!

Dwelling in the swamps and billabongs of Australia, the bunyip was a creature born from Aboriginal legend. After the arrival of the first Europeans, fears of the creature quickly spread throughout the settlements.

The monster was believed to live deep in the local waterholes, emerging only on moonlit nights in search of a meal of human flesh.

Although descriptions of the creature varied, all bunyips were said to have a deep, bellowing growl, fiery eyes and a huge body covered with fur or feathers. Eyewitnesses at Narrandera in New South Wales described a bunyip as 'about half as long again as an ordinary retriever dog. Hair all over its body, jet black and shining. Its coat, very long.' A group of three or four bunyips in Tasmania were described as being 'like a sheep dog about the head and from 3 to 5 feet long.' A Queenslander from Dalby, near Brisbane, gave a description of a bunyip he saw in 1873 as having 'a head like a seal and a tail consisting of two fins, a larger and a smaller one.'

In 1849, one astonished witness gave the following description: 'The animal, which was sitting on the bank of a lake, is described as being from 6 to 7 feet long and in general appearance, half man and half baboon. Five shots were fired and the last discharge was replied to by a spring into the air and a contemptuous fling-out of the hind legs and a final disappearance into the placid waters of the lake. A somewhat long neck, which was feathered like an emu, was the peculiar characteristic of the animal.'

Finally, there is this report from Ernestine Hill of Queensland, who reported a creature 'like a very large seal with a beard, and they say no one can catch it, even when the lakes are low, but a postal inspector once gave me a photograph of it. He explained that, while it showed up in the negative, it never showed up in the print, which confirmed the general belief that it was a chimerical beast'.

As with the legendary Loch Ness monster, the fabled deep-sea monster known as the Kraken and the mysterious Abominable Snowman (the giant man-beast of the Himalayas), Australia's bunyip remains elusive.

We may never fully know the truth of the bunyip's existence, but the poor creature would surely lose much of its charm as a folk legend should it one day decide to arise from its misty billabong and take a stroll through the suburbs, looking for a tasty snack of human meat.

Commas are used:

- to show a pause in a sentence. For example: *Listen, can you hear the thunder?*
- to separate a list of adjectives that describe a noun. For example: *She wore a pretty, red, spotty hat.* (No comma is needed after the final adjective that comes before the noun.)
- to separate words in a list. For example: *You need to take a scarf, gloves, a coat and a hat.*
- to separate main and subordinate clauses in a sentence. For example: *My uncle, who lives in Barrambat, will be coming to Brisbane for his holiday.*

1 Write commas to separate clauses in the following sentences from the text.

a Although descriptions of the creature varied all bunyips were said to have a deep, bellowing growl.

b Finally there is this report from Ernestine Hill of Queensland who reported a creature like a very large seal.

c Like the legendary Loch Ness monster Australia's bunyip remains elusive.

d After the arrival of the first Europeans fears of the creature quickly spread throughout the settlements.

e The animal which was sitting on the bank of a lake is described as being from 6 to 7 feet long.

f A somewhat long neck which was feathered like an emu was the peculiar characteristic of the animal.

2 Only one of the following sentences is correctly punctuated. Tick the box for the correctly punctuated sentence.

☐ The book, I am reading which is called *Bunyips Galore*, is hilarious.

☐ The book I am reading which is called, *Bunyips Galore*, is hilarious.

☐ The book I am reading, which is called *Bunyips Galore*, is hilarious.

☐ The book I am, reading which is called, *Bunyips Galore*, is hilarious.

3 Add commas, where needed, in the sentences below.

a When Mrs Argus came in she told us that she would be teaching our class again next year.

b Because it was raining the children decided to play inside.

c The clown was wearing big baggy yellow spotted pants.

d If you want to stay healthy eat apples strawberries and other tasty fruit.

CHALLENGE

Draw lines to match each kind of comma use with an example.

Comma use	Example
to separate items in a list	*"Wait here, I'll fetch your coat."*
to show a pause	*Some children, the ones who had waited patiently, were rewarded with gold medallions.*
to separate clauses	*Before us lay a dark, dismal, ominous sky.*
to separate adjectives	*We saw tigers, lions, cheetahs, leopards and a panther in the cats' enclosure.*

Comic capers

A HAGAR

Why do people call you 'Mean Max'?

It's just my appearance.

Why don't you try smiling more...you probably have a nice smile.

I am smiling.

B SWAGGLES

Where do you wash?

I wasn't asking when, I was asking where!

In the spring.

C PEANUTS

You should be out canoeing.

Why should I be out canoeing?

So you wouldn't be lying in my beanbag, about to be pounded, if you're not out in two seconds!

I wonder where they keep all the canoes...

© 1983 United Feature Syndicate, Inc.

OXFORD UNIVERSITY PRESS

Quoted (direct) speech shows words that are actually spoken.

For example: *"Have you finished washing up yet?" asked Mum.*

The actual words spoken by Mum are placed inside speech marks.

Reported (indirect) speech is a report of what has been said.

For example: *Mum asked if I had finished washing up yet.*

Speech marks are not used for indirect speech.

1 Underline the words actually spoken (**quoted speech**) in the following dialogue.

"Doctor, doctor," complained the patient, "I can't remember anything!"

"How long has this been going on?" asked Dr Green.

"How long has what been going on?" answered the bewildered patient.

2 Rewrite the following exchange in **quoted (direct) speech**.

A reporter asked the captain of a container ship if there were any vegetables he preferred not to carry. The captain answered that he was reluctant to carry leeks on his ship.

_____

_____

_____

_____

_____

Speech marks, inverted commas and quotation marks are all terms for the punctuation marks that enclose words that are actually spoken. They can be single or double, but they should be used consistently.

3 Think of a joke or riddle you know as **quoted (direct) speech** and write it as if you were telling it to your best friend.

_____

_____

_____

_____

CHALLENGE

On a separate piece of paper or a computer, write or type the 'Comic capers' on page 74 as both **quoted (direct)** and **reported (indirect)** speech.

General knowledge quiz

Conduct research, if necessary, to help you find and write the answers to these questions.

1 Which sport would you be playing if you'd just made a strike of 10?

_____

2 What won't a vegetarian eat?

_____

3 Who out of the following wasn't an outlaw? Ned Kelly, Jesse James, Robin Hood, Ironman, Ben Hall

_____

4 Name the position of any player in a netball team who isn't allowed to score goals.

_____

5 Which sportsperson would've achieved a Test match batting average of 100 if he had made just four more runs in his last Test?

_____

6 Which character doesn't belong? Bart, Lisa, Homer, Maggie, Peppa, Marge

_____

7 What's the name given to a person who assists a golfer?_____

8 Which of the following aren't crustaceans? crab, yabby, lobster, shark, seahorse, crayfish

_____

9 Who of the following weren't musical composers? Ludwig van Beethoven, Lennon & McCartney, Johann Sebastian Bach, Laurel & Hardy, Queen Elizabeth I, Wolfgang Amadeus Mozart, Luke Skywalker

_____

10 Name the cartoon character that's associated with the expression 'Doh!'

_____

OXFORD UNIVERSITY PRESS

An apostrophe of contraction is used to show that one or more letters have been left out of a word. For example: *can't = can not   I'd = I would or I had*

1 Use the text opposite to help you write the contractions (shortened forms) of these words.

a would have _____   b what is _____

c are not _____   d you had _____

e is not _____   f will not _____

g was not _____   h does not _____

i were not _____   j that is _____

2 Write these contractions in full.

a you're _____   b we've _____

c it's _____   d she'd _____

e they'd _____   f didn't _____

g could've _____   h don't _____

i you'll _____   j I'll _____

3 Rewrite the sentences giving the contractions in full.

a "I've never seen such a beautiful sight and I wouldn't expect to ever see anything that could compare," said the enthusiastic traveller.

_____

_____

b "If you can't be at my house by 10," said Rasheed irritably, "then we'll just have to miss the start of the game."

_____

_____

c She'd searched everywhere but she still couldn't find the list he'd given her.

_____

_____

Here are the quiz answers: 1 ten-pin bowling 2 meat 3 Ironman 4 Centre, Wing Attack, Wing Defence, Goal Defence and Goal Keeper 5 Sir Donald Bradman 6 Peppa 7 caddy 8 shark, seahorse 9 Laurel & Hardy, Queen Elizabeth 1 and Luke Skywalker 10 Homer Simpson

CHALLENGE

On a separate piece of paper or on a computer, write or type sentences that clearly show the difference in the meaning of the following words.

a *it's* and *its*   b *who's* and *whose*   c *we're* and *were*   d *you're* and *your*

Mixed-up possessions

Zorro's paintbrush

Robin Hood's helmet

Elizabeth's cape

Shirley Temple's footy

Superman's big ears

Ned Kelly's mask

Mickey Mouse's crown

Gazza's curls

Leonardo's bow and arrows

OXFORD UNIVERSITY PRESS

An apostrophe of possession is used to show that something belongs to a person or thing.
For example: *Erika's sword* = the sword belonging to Erika   *The wind's howl* = the howl of the wind

1 The possessions of the characters on the opposite page have become mixed up. Rewrite the following list correctly using **apostrophes of possession.**

a _____ helmet   b _____ big ears

c _____ cape   d _____ crown

e _____ mask   f _____ footy

g _____ curls   h _____ paintbrush

i _____ bow and arrows

When a word is singular, add an apostrophe and then add *s* whether the word ends in *s* or not.
For example: *The tractor's wheels were huge. James's dog is a collie.*

2 Rewrite using **apostrophes of possession.**

a the sails belonging to the ship _____

b the bicycle belonging to Charles _____

c the wail of the siren _____

d the cry of the wolf _____

When a word is plural, if it ends in *s* just add an apostrophe at the end of the word.
For example: *The horses' tails were swishing backwards and forwards.*

3 Rewrite using **apostrophes of possession.**

a the petals of the flowers _____

b the petals of the flower _____

c the buzz of the fly _____

d the buzz of the flies _____

> The easiest way to remember where to place an *apostrophe of possession* is to ask who the owner is. Once you know the owner, place the apostrophe after the last letter of the owner's name.

When a word is plural but does not end in *s*, add an apostrophe and then *s*.
For example: *The women's meeting was held in the new hall.*

4 Complete the following.

a the children_____ game   b the cattle_____ lowing

c the teeth_____ chatter   d the police_____ action

e the geese_____ feathers   f the men_____ room

CHALLENGE

On a separate piece of paper or on a computer, write or type the names of all of your family members – including pets – and your friends, as well as at least one possession they might have. For example: *Mum's Ford   Sparky's rubber bone   Sultan's saddle   Mia's footy*

Rangi and Papatua
(A Maori legend)

In the beginning, Rangi the sky father and Papatua the earth mother were so much in love that they hugged each other closely all the time.

When Rangi and Papatua's children were born, they were trapped in the darkness of their loving parents' embrace. The children didn't like living in such darkness all of the time so they decided that they should try to escape into the light.

First Rongo, who was the eldest child, tried to push his parents apart. He pushed and pushed but it was no good because Rangi and Papatua held each other too tightly.

Next Tangaroa tried. He heaved and pushed and strained, but he too failed to separate his parents. Each of the children took turns to separate their parents but without luck until finally it came to the youngest child, Tane, to try.

Tane placed his head upon earth mother Papatua's stomach. Then Tane placed his feet firmly into sky father Rangi's stomach. He pushed and strained and struggled as his brothers and sisters had done.

Rangi the sky father cried out, "Stop, my son!" but Tane continued to push.

Papatua the earth mother cried out, "Stop, my son!' but Tane continued to push.

Tane's parents began to shout and scream for they did not wish to be parted.

Slowly Tane began to stretch himself out and push his parents apart. Light started to stream into the world for the first time. The coming of light meant that plants began to grow.

Eventually Rangi and Papatua were parted, but they were so sad that they both began to cry. They cried and cried and their tears became the rivers, the lakes and the sea. They cried so much that their children thought their parents would flood the new world. The children decided to roll Papatua over for a short while each day so that Rangi couldn't see her. Once Rangi the sky father could no longer see his beloved wife, Papatua the earth mother, he stopped crying.

Today, when you wake up each morning you can see Rangi's tears in the form of dewdrops, which he sheds at the first sight of his wife. When Papatua sees Rangi for the first time each day she lets out loving sighs, which take the form of the early morning mists.

1 In each of the following sentences underline the **subject** in red and the **predicate** in blue.

    a Rongo tried to push his parents apart.

    b Tane's parents did not wish to be parted.

    c The tears became the rivers, lakes and the sea.

2 Circle the **verb** in brackets that agrees with the **subject**.

    a The children (was/were) trapped between their parents.

    b Tane (is/are) pushing and straining with all his might.

    c Their tears (become/became) the rivers, lakes and the sea.

3 Rewrite the following sentence elements to form one sensible sentence.

> placed (**verb**)   Tane (**subject**)   into Rangi's stomach (**phrase**)   his feet (**object**)

Remember, the subject is what is being talked about and the predicate is what is being said about the subject.

_____

4 Circle the **subordinating conjunction** in each of these sentences.

    a The children of Rangi and Papatua were trapped because of their loving parents' embrace.

    b Tane pushed and strained until he separated Rangi from Papatua.

    c The children of Rangi and Papatua loved their parents although they wished for more light.

5 Tick the sentence below that is punctuated correctly.

    a First Rongo who was the eldest child tried to push his parents apart.

    b First Rongo who was the eldest child, tried to push his parents apart.

    c First Rongo, who was the eldest child, tried to push his parents apart.

    d First, Rongo who was the eldest, child tried to push his parents apart.

6 Rewrite the following reported speech as **direct (quoted) speech**.

Rangi cried out that he wanted his son Tane to stop.

_____

CHALLENGE

On a separate piece of paper or on a computer, rewrite the following using apostrophes of possession where necessary.

    a the stomach of Rangi   **b** the children of Rangi and Papatua

    c the efforts of the children   **d** the tears of their parents

TOPIC 4: ASSESS YOUR GRAMMAR!

Sentences and punctuation

1 Shade the bubble next to the **subject** of the following sentence.

The sheep dog slowly circled the stray lambs.

○ The sheep dog   ○ slowly   ○ circled   ○ the stray lambs

2 Shade the bubble next to the **subject** of the following sentence.

The mayor announced excitedly that Toby was the winner.

○ The mayor   ○ announced excitedly

○ announced excitedly that Toby was the winner.   ○ Toby was the winner

3 Shade the bubble next to the correct answer and then write the answer in the box.

A subordinate clause can only be found in a [   ] .

○ simple sentence   ○ compound sentence   ○ complex sentence   ○ phrase

4 Shade the bubble next to the word that would correctly complete this sentence.

The singers [   ] *singing the national anthem.*

○ is   ○ are   ○ am   ○ was

5 Shade the bubble next to the word that would correctly complete this sentence.

Ally and Cam [   ] *eating ice cream.*

○ like   ○ likes   ○ lick   ○ liking

6 Shade the bubble next to the **object** in the following sentence.

Captain Swish carried the treasure chest.

○ Captain Swish   ○ carried   ○ the treasure chest   ○ carried the treasure chest

7 Shade the bubble next to the **prepositional phrase** in the following sentence.

The scout troop met at Black Dog Reserve.

○ The scout troop   ○ met   ○ at Black Dog Reserve   ○ The scout troop met

OXFORD UNIVERSITY PRESS

8 Shade the bubble below the **coordinating conjunction** in this sentence.

The girls had finished but the boys were still working.

○   ○   ○ ○

9 Shade the bubble next to the **subordinate conjunction** that would best join these sentences.

Harriet suspected the goblin was inside. The door was open.

○ where   ○ until   ○ although   ○ because

10 Mark where **commas** belong in this sentence.

The bear cub which had been slumbering peacefully awoke with a fright.

11 Shade the bubble next to the correctly punctuated sentence.

○ "Aren't you going to watch Perry's performance?" asked Coby's friend Tim.

○ Aren't you going to watch Perry's performance? "asked Coby's friend Tim."

○ "Are'nt you going to watch Perry's performance?" asked Coby's friend Tim.

○ "Aren't you going to watch Perrys' performance?" asked Cobys' friend Tim.

12 Shade the bubble that shows the **fleece of a sheep**.

○ a sheeps' fleece   ○ a sheeps fleece

○ a sheep's fleece   ○ a sheep fleece

13 Shade the bubble next to the **contraction** of **they are**.

○ there   ○ theyr'e   ○ their   ○ they're

TICK THE BOXES IF YOU UNDERSTAND.

A simple sentence contains one main clause made up of a subject and a predicate. ☐

The subject and verb of a sentence must agree. ☐

Coordinating and subordinating conjunctions are used to join clauses and simple sentences. ☐

Sentences can be simple, compound or complex. ☐

Commas can separate clauses in a sentence. ☐

Thunder and lightning

Do you know why we don't hear and see thunder and lightning at the same time? Read on to find out ...

Thunder is the sound lightning makes. Sound is made up of vibrations. These vibrations move through the air until they reach the ear. For us to be able to hear thunder, lightning must cause vibrations.

We know that lightning is a huge discharge of electricity. When this discharge takes place, the electricity hits the air and the air starts to vibrate. Lightning is also incredibly hot. The lightning heats up the air around it. Then the air expands because it is hot. This expanding air causes another vibration. These vibrations together bounce off clouds or the ground, causing the sound we hear as thunder.

The reason that we don't hear and see thunder and lightning at the same time is because light travels much faster than sound. This means that when you hear thunder the lightning that caused it has already occurred.

CAUSE	EFFECT
Lightning makes sound.	We hear thunder.
Vibrations move through the air.	The sound reaches our ear.
The vibration bounces off the air or the ground.	This causes the sound of thunder.
Light travels faster than sound.	We don't hear thunder and see lightning at the same time.

Facts about thunder and lightning

- Lightning can reach temperatures of 30 000°C, which is 5 times hotter than the surface of the Sun.
- Lightning strikes upwards as well as downwards.
- A stroke of lightning can be more than 30 kilometres long.
- Ball lightning is a really weird kind of lightning. It appears as a fiery, red, yellow or orange sphere, about the size of a grapefruit, which floats a metre or so above the ground.
- Scientists still don't fully understand how lightning works.

OXFORD UNIVERSITY PRESS

Let's look at the way grammar is used in an informative text. Informative texts, such as the explanation opposite, generally use a lot of complex sentences to explain how something happens or the reason why something occurs. A complex sentence contains a main clause and a subordinate clause starting with a subordinating conjunction.

Subordinate clauses can be added, where appropriate, to the start, the end or sometimes the middle of a main clause.

For example: Then, the air expands **because** it is hot.
Then, **because** it is hot, the air expands.
Because it is hot, the air expands.

Some common subordinating conjunctions include because, if, when, since, until and while.

1 Read 'Thunder and lightning'. Use the explanation on page 84 to help you rewrite the following complex sentences, placing the subordinate clause in an alternative place.

a Lightning must cause vibrations for us to be able to hear thunder.

_____

b Because light travels faster than sound, we don't hear thunder and see lightning at the same time.

_____

_____

2 Write three subordinating conjunctions that are used in the explanation on page 84 to join clauses.

_____   _____   _____

Informative texts, such as explanations, often include relating verbs written in the timeless present tense to show that the actions or states of being are continuous, always happening or always true. For example: *Thunder is the sound lightning makes.*

3 Write two sentences from the text on page 84 that are written in timeless present tense.

_____

_____

4 Write any relating verbs used in the sentences you wrote in Question 3.

_____

_____

5 Write three examples of technical nouns used in the explanation on page 84.

_____   _____   _____

CHALLENGE

Select one of the topics below and, on a separate piece of paper or on a computer, write or type an explanation of your own making sure you include complex sentences, timeless present tense, relating verbs and technical nouns.

Topics: • How paper is made.   • How a drone works.   • Believe it or not!

Tales from the Speewah

The Speewah is a mythical Australian station around which many tall tales of the bush are set. Alan Marshall, one such teller of bush yarns, had the following to say about life on the Speewah.

… Firstly, there is 'Crooked Mick' who tried to strangle himself with his own beard in the Big Drought. He was a gun shearer; five hundred a day was nothing to him. Once, the boss, annoyed because of Crooked Mick's rough handling of some wethers, strode up to him on the board and barked, "You're fired!" Crooked Mick was shearing flat out at the time. He was going so fast that he shore fifteen sheep before he could straighten up and hang his shears on the hook …

… The kangaroos there were as tall as mountains and the emus laid eggs that men blew and used for houses …

… The Speewah holding itself was a tremendous size. When Uncle Harry was sent out to close the garden gate he had to take a week's rations with him. A jackeroo, going out to bring in the cows from the horse paddock, was gone for six months …

… Hundreds of men worked on the Speewah. In fact, there were so many, they had to mix the mustard with a long-handled shovel and the cook and his assistant had to row out in a boat to sugar the tea …

… The Speewah was cursed with every plague. Rabbits were so thick you had to pull them out of the burrows to get the ferrets in and trappers had to brush them aside to set their traps. On some of the paddocks they had to drive them out to get room to put the sheep in.

from *How's Andy Going?* by Alan Marshall

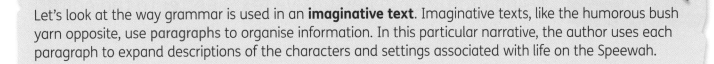

Let's look at the way grammar is used in an **imaginative text**. Imaginative texts, like the humorous bush yarn opposite, use paragraphs to organise information. In this particular narrative, the author uses each paragraph to expand descriptions of the characters and settings associated with life on the Speewah.

1 Read the humorous text on page 86, then write a label that could be used to describe the main subject or topic of each paragraph.

First paragraph _Crooked Mick_   Fourth paragraph _____

Second paragraph _____   Fifth paragraph _____

Third paragraph _____

Prepositional phrases often feature in imaginative texts to sharpen ideas and develop a fuller description of the details about how, when and where things are taking place.

2 Complete the sentences below with prepositional phrases from page 86. Beside each sentence, write whether the phrase tells **how**, **when** or **where**.

   a Crooked Mick tried to strangle himself **with** _____

   b Crooked Mick was shearing flat out **at** _____

   c The jackeroo brought in the cows **from** _____

   d The Speewah was cursed **with** _____

The authors of imaginative bush yarns often play with language to entertain their audience. In this case, Alan Marshall has used humorous sentences, playful exaggerations and even a simile in his descriptions to entertain his audience.

3 Use different colours to underline some of the humorous sentences and exaggerated descriptions Alan Marshall has used in this bush yarn.

4 Write the simile used in the bush yarn to describe the kangaroos that lived on the Speewah.

_____

5 Rewrite the sentence below, replacing the saying verb in bold with the more specific saying verb the author uses to demonstrate the type of character Mick's boss was.

"You're fired!" **said** Mick's boss. _____

CHALLENGE

On a separate piece of paper or on a computer, write or type an imaginative Speewah tall tale of your own by using the following to help you.

The wombats on the Speewah were so big that ...   _Crooked Mick was so strong that ..._

Ned Kelly – hero or villain?

Recently an article appeared in the *Nor'easter* newspaper about the bushranger Ned Kelly. A number of people responded to the article with letters to the editor debating whether the outlaw was an Australian hero or villain. Here is the latest letter …

Dear Editor,

I cannot let Sally Thornton's letter to your newspaper, dated 16/1/2020, go unanswered because all the facts definitely point to Ned Kelly being a villain, not a hero. Let me cite to Ms Thornton some of these facts.

First, as a teen, Kelly was an apprentice to Harry Powers, which sounds commendable, until you become aware that Powers was a horse thief! The young villain went on to become accomplished at stealing horses, at the same time establishing a reputation around north-east Victoria as a bare-knuckle brawler. This makes him a thief and a thug.

Second, let me remind you of the indisputable fact that Kelly and his sidekicks were responsible for the cold-blooded murder of three police officers at Stringybark Creek. Kelly, after stealing the watch from the dead Sergeant Kennedy, is quoted as saying, "What's the use of a watch to a dead man?" This surely leaves no doubt that Kelly was a remorseless murderer.

Then, there is the siege at the Glenrowan Hotel in which Kelly and his gang of thugs held innocent civilians hostage. Around the same time, the gang attempted to derail a train carrying police troops and their horses. This makes Kelly a nineteenth-century terrorist.

Next, let us not forget that in the lead-up to the siege at Glenrowan, Kelly had despatched Joe Byrne to murder his boyhood friend and suspected police informer, Aaron Sherritt. Sherritt was unarmed and with his wife and newly born babe when Byrne gunned him down. This makes Kelly and Byrne vengeful bullies.

In summary, Sally, let the facts speak for themselves. Rather than set Ned Kelly high up on that hero's pedestal to be worshipped and adored, we really should be remembering him for exactly what he was – a notorious and villainous killer.

Prof. J. S. Providence (Melbourne, Australia)

OXFORD UNIVERSITY PRESS

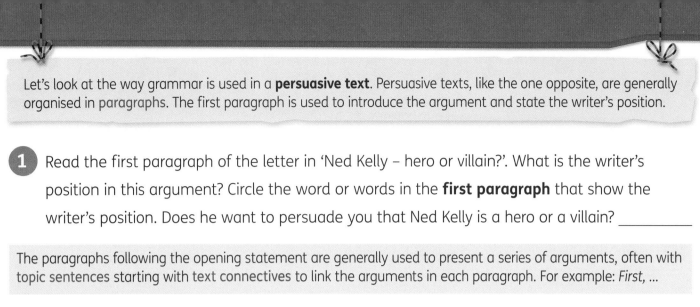

Let's look at the way grammar is used in a **persuasive text**. Persuasive texts, like the one opposite, are generally organised in paragraphs. The first paragraph is used to introduce the argument and state the writer's position.

1 Read the first paragraph of the letter in 'Ned Kelly – hero or villain?'. What is the writer's position in this argument? Circle the word or words in the **first paragraph** that show the writer's position. Does he want to persuade you that Ned Kelly is a hero or a villain? _____

The paragraphs following the opening statement are generally used to present a series of arguments, often with topic sentences starting with text connectives to link the arguments in each paragraph. For example: *First, …*

2 Read the rest of the letter to the editor, then write the text connectives used to link the paragraphs.

_____

3 Write one example of a topic sentence used to introduce the main idea of a paragraph.

_____

In this persuasive text, the writer has carefully selected specific noun groups to portray the main character in a negative light to further persuade the audience of his point of view.

4 Write the noun groups in each paragraph that are used to describe Ned Kelly.

First paragraph: *a villain*

Second paragraph: _____

Third paragraph: _____

Fourth paragraph: _____

Fifth paragraph: _____

Concluding paragraph: _____

5 Write the antonym for *villain* used in contrast to Ned Kelly. _____

6 Write two modal adverbs used on page 88. _____

Write a letter to the editor about someone you regard as a hero. Use specific noun groups to portray your hero in a positive manner in order to persuade your audience that he or she is deserving of an award.

OR: Argue one side or discuss both sides of one of the following arguments:

- Should professional sport be played on Anzac Day?
- Is climate change real?
- Chicken farming – caged or free range?

Punctuation

1 Shade the bubble next to the missing punctuation mark to complete the sentence.

What a fantastic hat

○ .   ○ ?   ○ !   ○ ,

2 Shade the bubble next to the missing punctuation mark to complete the sentence.

We travelled from Cairns to Brisbane

○ .   ○ ?   ○ !   ○ ,

3 Shade the bubble next to the missing punctuation mark to complete the sentence.

Where did you find your locket

○ .   ○ ?   ○ !   ○ ,

4 Shade the bubble next to the correctly punctuated sentence.

○ Is the city with the largest population in england london.

○ Is the city with the largest population in England, London?

○ Is the city with the largest population in England, London.

○ Is the city with the largest population in england, London?

5 Shade the bubble next to the correctly punctuated sentence.

○ The rainbow's colours are violet, indigo, blue, green, yellow, orange and red.

○ The rainbow's, colours are violet indigo blue green yellow orange and red.

○ The rainbow's colours are, violet indigo blue green yellow orange and red.

○ The rainbow's, colours, are, violet, indigo, blue, green, yellow, orange and red.

6 Shade the bubble next to the correctly punctuated sentence.

○ Magda who had only just arrived sat down next to Sadie.

○ Magda, who had only just arrived, sat down next to Sadie.

○ Magda who, had only just arrived, sat down next to Sadie.

○ Magda who had only just arrived, sat down next to Sadie.

7 Shade the bubble next to the correctly punctuated sentence.

○ Look out shouted Tom who had been watching Mel with interest.

○ Look out "shouted Tom!" who had been watching Mel with interest.

○ "Look out!" shouted Tom, who had been watching Mel with interest.

○ "Look out!" shouted Tom, "who had been watching Mel with interest."

8 Use the correct punctuation to rewrite this sentence in the box.

A flat long hard throw is much better than a high soft one explained our coach

9 Add commas, where they belong, in this sentence.

The dancers who had been rehearsing for weeks performed splendidly.

10 Shade the bubble next to the correctly punctuated sentence.

○ "Hey, let's eat Grandad!"   ○ "Hey, let's eat, Grandad!"

○ "Hey let's eat Grandad!"   ○ "Hey let,s eat Grandad!"

TICK THE BOXES IF YOU UNDERSTAND.

I understand how grammar is used in informative (explanation), imaginative and persuasive texts. ☐

I understand how to use grammar to enrich and improve what I write. ☐

UNIT 6.1   Prefixes and suffixes

Fabulous monsters **2**

The Lernean Hydra

From Greek mythology, the Hydra was a huge serpent living in the Lernean Swamp. The monster had many heads (some say seven and some say nine), each of which breathed poisonous breath. The Lernean Hydra was confronted by the courageous hero Heracles, who found that when he lopped one head from the massive creature, two more grew in its place. To overcome the problem of multiple heads growing, Heracles used a torch to seal each neck stump shut so no further heads could grow.

One of the heads, however, was immortal and, upon lopping it from the creature's neck, Heracles imprisoned it beneath a massive rock. There it may very well be even today.

The Kraken

Scandinavian mythologies tell us of a huge, tentacled sea monster resembling a giant squid. It is said to be so large that it can be mistaken for a small island. Spending most of its time slumbering in the deepest parts of the ocean, the Kraken occasionally awakens, stirs and arises to the surface to attack ships by wrapping its massive tentacles around vessels and crushing them or dragging both them and their crews down into the murky depths.

It is thought that the stories about the Kraken are based on the sightings of real giant squid which, although not the size of small islands, are still capable of wrestling a sperm whale and capsizing a small fishing boat.

OXFORD UNIVERSITY PRESS

Prefixes are word parts that change the meaning of words when added to the beginning of another word or word part.
For example: *inter-* means 'between' or 'among' (*intersect, internet, intermediate*)

1 Add prefixes from the box to the words or word parts to form new words.

> tele-   fore-   anti-   mono-

a _____clockwise   b _____plane   c _____leg

d _____scope   e _____phone   f _____head

g _____nuclear   h _____rail   i _____vision

2 Add prefixes to the following words to make them antonyms (opposites).

a _____visible   b _____fortunate   c _____appear

d _____knowingly   e _____perfect   f _____behave

g _____responsible   h _____legal   i _____sense

Suffixes are word endings. When some suffixes are added to nouns or verbs, they usually form adjectives.
For example: *break + able = breakable, sense + ible = sensible, glory + ous = glorious*

3 Use suffixes or prefixes to change the following nouns to adjectives.

a poison _____   b mortal _____

c remark _____   d courage _____

4 Write your own words that can begin with the following prefixes.

a **tri-** *(meaning three)* _____

b **bi-** *(meaning two)* _____

c **auto-** *(meaning self)* _____

_____

CHALLENGE

The suffix -ist means 'person who does'. Write 10 words ending in -ist that describe people who do things. For example: *artist* (someone who works in any of the arts). On a separate piece of paper or on a computer, write a sentence for each word.

_____   _____   _____   _____   _____

_____   _____   _____   _____   _____

The shark

He seemed to know the harbour,

So leisurely he swam;

His fin,

Like a piece of sheet-iron,

Three-cornered,

And with a knife-edge,

Stirred not a bubble

As it moved

With its base-line on the water.

His body was tubular

And tapered

And smoke-blue,

And as he passed the wharf

He turned,

And snapped at a flat-fish

That was dead and floating.

And I saw the flash of a white throat,

And a double row of white teeth,

And eyes of metallic grey,

Hard and narrow and slit.

Then out of the harbour,

With that three-cornered fin,

Shearing without a bubble the water

Lithely,

Leisurely,

He swam -

That strange fish,

Tubular, tapered, smoke-blue,

Part vulture, part wolf,

Part neither – for his blood was cold.

E. J. Pratt

OXFORD UNIVERSITY PRESS

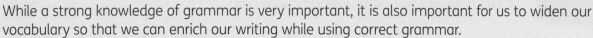

While a strong knowledge of grammar is very important, it is also important for us to widen our vocabulary so that we can enrich our writing while using correct grammar.

1 Use the poem on page 94 and the parts of speech listed to help you find interesting words that mean the following.

a *(adverb)* at a relaxed and easy pace _____

b *(verb)* slicing through _____

c *(adjective)* shaped like a tube _____

d *(common noun)* a scavenging bird of prey _____

e *(adjective)* like metal _____

f *(verb)* agitated _____

g *(noun)* place where boats dock _____

h *(adjective)* triangular _____

2 Use a dictionary to help you write clear definitions for these words.

a lithely _____

b tapered _____

c dorsal fin _____

3 Write words from the poem on page 94 that are **antonyms** for these words.

a alive _____   **b** sinking _____

c wide _____   **d** frantically _____

CHALLENGE

The words in the box below are all **abstract nouns** of emotion.
Circle the **abstract nouns** that you think best describe how the poet felt about the shark.

sadness	excitement	apprehension	nervousness	anger	fear
panic	terror	shame	alarm	jealousy	sorrow
pity	awe	fury	boredom	love	depression
wonder	interest	embarrassment			

Jordy's postcard

Jordy has been travelling in the wilds of Canada. After a close encounter, he decided to be a bit old-fashioned and send a postcard to Rema, his friend in Australia. Unfortunately, Jordy didn't pay much attention in his English classes back home. Can you decipher what he has written on his postcard home?

Deer rema,

Isle bee home soon.

   Your knot going two believe watt Im going too tell yew. Yesterday in the woulds near the creak I sore too bares. Won was a mail I think because he had grate big pause. Anyways, both the bares clause was huge. I thought they had mist seaing me but suddenly the won I thought was a mail let out a whale and rushed strait four me. Luckily I was able two seas hold of a low bow and swing up into a nearby beach tree. That bare beet the trunk with his pores but I scrambled hire and was safe. I no in future daze to come ill take moor care when im bye myself. I is looking forward to catching up and sharing sum other storeys with ewe when I return to australia in a few weaks thyme.

   Youre good friend jordy.

1 As you have seen on page 96, Jordy's postcard needs a little bit of work before it can be easily read.

Edit Jordy's postcard for him by rewriting it below.

Look out for homonyms, incorrect contractions and poor punctuation.

_____

_____

_____

_____

_____

_____

_____

_____

_____

_____

_____

_____

_____

_____

_____

_____

_____

_____

_____

_____

_____

_____

_____

Slip ... slipping away

Did you know that frogs have survived on our planet for nearly 200 million years? Humans, however, in our modern form, have been here for only 200 000 years. Unfortunately, there is evidence that frog populations are quickly diminishing, which has alarmed many scientists. Entire frog species are also at risk of extinction. This should be of great concern to us all because it is known that the elements that affect the existence of frogs – air, water and the earth – are the same elements that affect human existence. Many believe that if frog extinction is inevitable, then human extinction is probably inevitable as well.

There are many factors contributing to the frightening decline of frog populations around the world.

Climate change

Global warming is a serious threat to all species of frogs.

Habitat destruction

Deforestation worldwide, the draining of marshes for human settlement and the damming of waterways mean certain death for many frog species.

Disease

The disease *Chytrid* is a fungal disease which is normally only associated with plants. The disease now, however, seems to have singled out small vertebrate species, and frogs are at the top of the list of potential victims.

Pollution

Frogs' skin and eggs are extremely permeable (easily allowing fluid to soak in). This means that many frogs absorb toxic substances such as acid rain, pesticides and other agricultural chemicals used by humans.

Interspecies competition

Non-native fish have been introduced into our river systems for food and recreation. These fish compete fiercely with native frogs for food as well as preying on them directly.

There are many other factors to consider when reflecting on the demise of our little amphibian friends. Perhaps the words of scientific researcher Steve Walker from the University of Adelaide should be closely heeded. He said that frogs survived whatever killed the dinosaurs. If they're starting to disappear because of humans, that's a real cause for concern.

GOING GOING GOING GOING POOF!

OXFORD UNIVERSITY PRESS

1 Circle the three common nouns in this sentence.

Frogs have survived on our planet longer than humans.

2 Circle the two adjectives in this sentence.

The fungal disease Chytrid has been attacking small vertebrates.

3 Circle the verbs or verb groups in these sentences.

a   Frogs are disappearing very quickly.

b   Many frogs absorb toxic substances.

c   Non-native fish have been introduced into our river systems.

4 Circle the adverb in this sentence.

Frogs' skin and eggs are extremely permeable.

5 Rewrite the following sentences as one sentence using a conjunction to join them. In your new sentence, replace any repeated common nouns with suitable pronouns.

Frogs disappearing is alarming for all of us.

It is known that what affects frogs also affects humans.

_____

_____

6 Underline the prepositional phrase in this sentence.

Non-native fish have been introduced into our river systems.

7 Write commas where they belong in the following sentence.

Climate change habitat destruction disease pollution and interspecies

competition are all threatening the existence of frogs.

CHALLENGE

Rewrite the reported (indirect) speech of scientist Steve Walker on page 98 as quoted (direct) speech using the correct punctuation.

_____

_____

_____

TIME TO REFLECT

Tick or shade the boxes when you are confident that you understand and can use the grammar listed.

Grammar and punctuation focus	Understand	Use
I select specific common, proper, collective or abstract nouns to represent people, places, things and ideas.		
I choose suitable nouns to fit the topic of my writing or to represent different characters or settings.		
I use a range of adjectives to describe characters and settings.		
I know how to expand noun groups with articles and a variety of adjectives for fuller descriptions.		
I use thinking and feeling verbs to express opinions.		
I use modal verbs like **could**, **would**, **should** and **must** to help persuade my audience.		
I choose suitable doing, saying or relating verbs to report facts or entertain the reader.		
I can use present, past and future tense verbs correctly.		
I use adverbs and prepositional phrases to make interesting sentences with details about where, when, how or why something happens.		
I use antonyms (opposites) and synonyms (words with a similar meaning) to help describe and compare people, places, things or ideas.		
I use paragraphs to organise my writing into logical bundles.		
I use topic sentences to introduce the main idea in each paragraph.		
I use pronouns that agree with the noun to which they refer. For example: **Evie/she, the boys/they**		

Grammar and punctuation focus	Understand	Use
I know how to use text connectives to link paragraphs or sentences in time or sequence. For example: **first, then, later, finally**		
I sometimes use similes in my writing to describe and compare subjects or to develop a character or setting.		
I know how to use coordinating conjunctions (**and, but, so, or**) to make a compound sentence.		
I know how to use the subordinating conjunctions (for example: **if, because, until, when**) to join a main clause to a subordinate clause.		
I know the difference between simple, compound and complex sentences.		
I understand that the subject and verb in a sentence must agree.		
I recognise how quotation marks are used in quoted (direct) speech.		
I understand the difference between quoted (direct) and reported (indirect) speech.		
I use commas in lists correctly most of the time.		
I understand that an apostrophe of contraction can be used to show where a letter is missing in a shortened word.		
I understand how to use an apostrophe of possession to show ownership.		

GLOSSARY

adjective	A word that describes a noun: *red, old, large, round, three* comparative adjective (compares two things): *stronger* positive adjective (in simplest form): *strong, good* superlative adjective (compares more than two things): *strongest, best, most enjoyable*
adverb	A word that usually adds meaning to a verb to tell when, where or how something happened: *slowly, immediately, soon, here* modal adverb (shows degree of certainty): *definitely, probably*
antonym	An opposite: *full/empty, sitting/standing, front/back*
apostrophe of contraction	A punctuation mark that shows where a letter (or letters) is missing in a contraction (shortened word): *isn't, we'll*
apostrophe of possession	A punctuation mark that shows ownership: *Ali's hat, the woman's car, the students' backpacks*
clause	A unit of grammar that usually contains a subject and a verb. There are main clauses and subordinate clauses. *When Peter called out, I looked around.*
comma	A punctuation mark used to separate items in a list, to show a short pause or to separate a main clause and a subordinate clause. *Mum, can I go? When I leave, I will take some apples, bananas, oranges and cherries.*
coordinating conjunction	A joining word used to join two simple sentences or main ideas: *and, but, so, or*
homograph	A word that is spelled the same but has a different meaning: *saw* (a tool), *saw* (past tense of *see*)
homonym	A word that looks or sounds the same: *Wind the window out and let the wind in.*
homophone	A word that sounds the same but is spelled differently: *sun/son*
metaphor	A figure of speech that compares something as if it were that thing: *The night was a cloak; the grapefruit moon*

noun	A word that names people, places, animals, things or ideas. Nouns can be: **abstract nouns** (things that cannot be seen or touched): *happiness, idea* **collective nouns** (names a group): *team, flock, bunch, herd* **common nouns** (names of ordinary things): *hat, toys, pet, mouse, clock, bird* **concrete nouns** (things that can be seen or touched): *book, pet, boy, girl* **proper nouns** (special names): *Max, Perth, Friday, March, Easter, Australia* **technical nouns** (sometimes called scientific nouns): *oxygen*
noun group	A group of words, often including an article, one or more adjectives and a noun, built around a main noun: *the strange, old house*
paragraph	A section of text containing a number of sentences about a particular point. Each paragraph starts on a new line.
plural	More than one: *chairs, dishes, boxes, cities, donkeys, loaves, foci*
predicate	What is being said about the thing or person (subject) in a sentence.
prefix	A word part that, when added to the beginning of another word or word part, changes the meaning: **dis**appear, **mis**behave
preposition	A word that usually begins a prepositional phrase: *on, in, over, under, before*
prepositional phrase	A group of words that starts with a preposition and adds details about when, where, how, why: *in the car, after lunch, with a spoon, for Olivia*
pronoun	A word that can take the place of a noun to represent a person, place or thing: *he, she, I, it* **first person pronoun**: *I, me, mine, we, us, ours* **possessive pronoun**: *mine, his, hers, ours, yours, theirs* **relative pronoun**: *who, whom, whose, which, that* **second person pronoun**: *you, yours* **third person pronoun**: *he, him, his, she, her, hers, it, its, they, them, theirs*
quoted (direct) speech	The direct speech that someone actually says. Quoted speech uses quotation marks at the start and end of the actual words spoken.
reported (indirect) speech	The indirect speech reporting what someone else has said.
sentence	A group of words that makes sense, and includes a subject and at least one verb. A **simple sentence** has one main idea or main clause and one verb or verb group: *The birds were sitting on the fence.* A **compound sentence** uses coordinating conjunctions (*and, but, or, so*) to join two main clauses. A compound sentence has two verbs or verb groups: *Some birds were sitting on the fence and a cat was lurking below.*

	A complex sentence uses subordinating conjunctions to join a main clause with one or more subordinate clauses. A complex sentence has two or more verbs or verb groups: *The tiger snake eats birds, although frogs are its preferred prey.*
simile	A figure of speech used to compare two things using the words *like* or *as*: *like a bird; as red as a beetroot*
subject	The noun or noun group naming who or what a sentence is about.
subordinating conjunction	A joining word used to join a main clause and one or more subordinate clauses: *because, since, when, if*
suffix	A word ending. They often change the part of speech of a word: *grace – graceful*
synonym	A word that means the same or nearly the same as another word: *shouts/yells, thin/skinny*
text connective	A signpost word or group of words that tells how the text is developing – generally used to link two sentences or paragraphs: *First, Second, Next, However, For instance*
topic sentence	A sentence, usually placed at the start of a paragraph, that introduces the main point being made in the paragraph.
verb	A word that tells us what is happening in a sentence. Verbs can be: auxiliary verbs (helping verbs used with a main verb): **is** *going,* **could** *go* compound verbs (made up of a helper, or auxiliary, and main verb): *is sitting* doing verbs: *walked, swam* modal verbs (telling how sure we are about doing something): *should, could, would, may, might, must, can, will, shall* relating verbs: *am, is, are, had* saying verbs: *said, asked* simple verbs (one word): *went* thinking and feeling verbs: *know, like*
verb group	A group of words built around a head word that is a verb: *might have been wondering*
verb tense	Refers to time and tells whether the action or process is in the present, past or future: *runs/is running, thought/was thinking, will help* timeless present tense: Used when the action is continuous: *Flies are insects.*

OXFORD UNIVERSITY PRESS